THE
TREE-SITTER

ALSO BY SUZANNE MATSON

FICTION
A Trick of Nature
The Hunger Moon

POETRY
Durable Goods
Sea Level

THE
TREE-SITTER
a novel

SUZANNE MATSON

W. W. Norton & Company New York London

Excerpt from "A narrow fellow in the grass" by Emily Dickinson reprinted by
permission of the publishers and the Trustees of Amherst College from *The Poems of
Emily Dickinson: Reading Edition*, Ralph W. Franklin, ed., Cambridge, Mass.: The
Belknap Press of Harvard University Press, copyright © 1998, 1999 by the
President and Fellows of Harvard College.

For information about permission to reproduce selections from this book, write to
Permissions, W. W. Norton & Company, Inc., 500 Fifth Avenue, New York, NY 10110

Manufacturing by Courier Westford
Book design by Anna Oler

Library of Congress Cataloging-in-Publication Data

Matson, Suzanne, date.
The tree-sitter : a novel / Suzanne Matson. — 1st ed.
p. cm.
ISBN 0-393-06046-2 (hardcover)
1. Women environmentalists—Fiction. 2. Women college students—Fiction.
3. Forest conservation—Fiction. 4. Ecoterrorism—Fiction. 5. Oregon—Fiction.
I. Title.
PS3563.A8378T74 2006
813'.54—dc22
2005024355

W. W. Norton & Company, Inc., 500 Fifth Avenue, New York, N.Y. 10110
www.wwnorton.com

W. W. Norton & Company Ltd., Castle House, 75/76 Wells Street, London W1T 3QT

1 2 3 4 5 6 7 8 9 0

For Joe, Nick, Henry, and Teddy

ACKNOWLEDGMENTS

For their generous readings and suggestions that have helped to make this a better book, I am grateful to Suzanne Berne, Jill Bialosky, Henry Dunow, and Elizabeth Graver. For fellowship support that provided the essential gift of time to write, I thank Boston College. My research into the forest protection movement was aided by two cogent and comprehensive studies: *The Final Forest: The Battle for the Last Great Trees of the Pacific Northwest*, by William Dietrich; and *Tree Huggers: Victory, Defeat and Renewal in the Northwest Ancient Forest Campaign*, by Kathie Durbin. As always, Joe Donnellan has been an indispensable ally in life and in work; and Nick, Henry, and Teddy have provided me with daily and incontrovertible evidence that our environmental legacies will matter profoundly. Finally, I am indebted to a masked young man named Wily Coyote who obligingly lowered himself out of an old-growth Douglas Fir in the Willamette National Forest to show me the ropes.

Several of Nature's People
I know, and they know me—
I feel for them a transport
Of cordiality—

But never met this Fellow
Attended, or alone
Without a tighter breathing
And Zero at the Bone—

—Emily Dickinson

1

In the beginning, I had to learn patience from the tree itself. That summer, '99, a cusp of things—for me, at least, the last spell of innocence—I discovered a quietude inside. Though that quiet is largely missing now, it's not entirely gone. I can still sometimes conjure the immensity of being there, of feeling time as encircling rings that link me to the past, the present, and—I have to believe—the future.

At 150 feet in the air, you're higher than a ten-story building. But your view down is partial, filtered; it's not the unobstructed arrogance of the penthouse or the corner office. Perched on a plywood platform in the branches of an old-growth Douglas Fir, you feel the tree alive beneath you. You're part of a tapestry of forest branches and slanted, always changing light. There is no feeling of towering *over*, but of being woven into the tree's purpose and place.

I was afraid to climb at first. But the rule was you couldn't stay at base camp unless you were prepared to take one action per twenty-four hours. And I wanted to stay. I'd come for Neil, whom I was trying to learn to call River. Name yourself, they told me the first night, and introduced me to their world: Mole, Slippery, Hellcat, Brave, Spiderman, Doe, Cougar, Mudman, Squirrel, Starling, Rain. What's the opposite of anthropomorphic? We weren't trying to project ourselves onto the animals and land-scape, we were trying to lose ourselves in them, wear their names. Erase the greedy, grasping DNA of the human and assume our role as part of an intricate, mysterious system. Goodbye, Julie—high school valedictorian, Wellesley student, rule-following daughter of Ginnie Prince, who was founding partner of Prince Baylor. It took one new name to leave Julie Prince behind, to slip loose from my mother's world of law. "I want Julie to do whatever she wants," my mother was fond of saying to her friends when they discussed children. "It's no use unless she finds something she loves," the friends would agree, nodding like unusually pleas-ant and permissive Sisters of the Fates. "Of course, college comes first," my mother would hasten to add. "Graduate school can wait until she's sure." My mother loves telling people how wise she was to take a few years off between Wellesley and law school—one year for traveling Europe, two years in the Peace Corps—part of JFK's initial idealistic wave—and a stint working on political cam-paigns. Her escapes were not so much rebellions as they were résumé-builders, shaped to the academic calendar and underwrit-ten by family money.

Name myself. Everything that passed through my senses was a possible name, a potential key to my new self. The evening we arrived in the forest I leaned against Neil—always Neil to me, I have to admit, even when he was supposed to be his alias—and watched the flames dance in the campfire. *Smoke. Ember.* The joints went around the circle and I inhaled the sweet burning and passed the roach thinking, *Weed. Grass.* I lay on my back on the sleeping bag being fucked by him—his word for it, I used no word until he taught me to say it, then like the sound of it. *Stone,* hard and resisting, fist in the small of my back. *Moon. Cloud. Star.* Or, more poetic, *Luna, Cirrus, Andromeda.* I followed Andromeda into other myth names—*Echo, Persephone, Diana,* and I especially liked the idea of being stolen from the mother or the part about becoming the tree itself, but in the end those stories called to mind visions that were too powerless, too captive, too gendered. My mother would be proud of me for that. She liked to call me "Jules" for short, liking, no doubt, the nickname's androgynous, Amazonian overtones. But I heard "Jewels" when I was a little girl, and I could never get rid of that notion of myself as treasure. As something to be gained or lost, found or buried. Owned.

It wasn't until dawn, when I woke to the dew-soaked edges of our sleeping bag and a deafening chatter of birds, that I hit upon it. The sun streaming through the lacework of the forest canopy was green, glowing like underwater light. For a minute I lost my sense of direction; looking up felt like looking down. *Emerald.* I wanted to dissolve into that greenness, be a part of it. Emerald: jewel, yes. A richness to hold safe and give away simultaneously, using our bodies as collateral to keep the fretwork of ancient trees out of the jaws of the logging industry.

Emerald! It sounds ridiculous now, but I felt born into that morning and that palpable light. I burrowed into Neil, who, overnight, had decided to become River. Later, on our platform, hours and hours to kill, I asked him about choosing it, and he told me about wanting to be part of the rush and power he'd felt when first rafting the Snake River. Long, slow bends whipsawed by sudden rapids that could throw you from your raft in an instant. Whitewater churning against your paddles and lashing you into rocks. That's the kind of force Neil wanted from his name.

The whole movement was made of names. Someone called us Ewoks after the *Star Wars* creatures who—I never saw the movie, but I was told—lived in trees and rebelled against the Empire. We named our tree villages, our platforms, the very trees—*Sawtooth, Fog, Laughing Man*. Like Adams and Eves, we claimed paradise by naming it. I suppose that's the human thing to do. But I see how I contradict myself already: We did project ourselves, how could we not? Without names there was no knowing the territory, no mapping our positions in the war. For eventually it was a war, though at first it was simply paradise.

So, Emerald, which everyone soon shortened to Em, and which I later signed as M when I scribbled a note to Neil or Mole. By then I preferred the unknowable M, with her sharp points and lack of signifier, to the romantic Emerald, embarrassingly linked to Oz and childhood jewelry boxes with those infinitely spinning, single-melodied ballerinas.

2

nlikely, that my journey to the forest started at a frat party, surrounded by Sloan School types. But that's where I found Neil, sitting on the floor, engrossed in conversation with a couple of others, while around them people were playing some game that involved everyone taking turns drinking as fast and as much as they could. I poured myself a cup of beer from the keg and positioned myself on the arm of a ratty old couch, close to the interesting guys. What drew me was their intensity, their focus. Everyone else at the party had the fixed look of glazed hilarity teetering toward oblivion. I didn't go to many frat parties and wasn't having fun at this one—I'd come only at the urging of my roommate Frida, who was there at the invitation of a guy she'd met once at another party.

I wasn't having any luck listening in on the conversation over the blasting of Pearl Jam, so I settled for watching their faces. Neil's especially. The tilt of his head when he listened, the way he'd cock an eyebrow skeptically, the silent nodding he'd do through someone's point when you could tell he'd already anticipated what they were going to say. I could see he was smart, but I could also see that he was a person who cared about things; his wasn't a casual face. His longish hair was so dark it was almost black, and his brown eyes had thick, expressive brows above them. He wore torn jeans and a flannel shirt washed to a buttery softness, and I later learned that these were all he would wear—whether to his dissertation defense, or to meet my mother, or to a tree-sit. Just when I'd given up on hearing anything and was thinking I'd tap Frida and tell her I was ready to go, he raised his eyes above the guy who was speaking and smiled at me. It was a smile that said everything—that he knew I'd been waiting there, that he only needed to finish listening to the friend who was speaking before he could rise up from his position on the floor and come sit by me.

In a few minutes he clapped one hand on the other guy's shoulder as a kind of final punctuation mark, used it to give himself leverage to stand up, and came over and sat down on the couch next to me. Instead of the red plastic party cup the rest of us clutched, he'd managed to find a bottle of Dos Equis. He looked at me, his face lively with amusement.

"You're not having fun," he said.

"Not yet."

"You know anyone here?"

"Frida." I pointed at her across the room. She was leaning against the boy she had a crush on. He had his arms wrapped around her, so I could see things were moving right along.

He smiled again, extending his hand. "Neil. And you?"

"Julie."

"Well, Julie. You don't like to play Beer Pong."

"No."

"Then you probably don't want to wait around for another hour until they start the Flip Cup tournament."

I made a face.

"Want to take a walk?"

I was already sure that I wanted to sleep with him. I wasn't promiscuous, never let myself be pressured into anything I didn't want to do. But my sexual radar was reliable. If I was attracted to someone in the first few minutes, the feeling would last. It had something to do with whether a guy was able to see me a certain way. There had to be a searching quality to his eyes, then some spark of recognition. He had to be looking for me, too.

Frida was happy I was taken care of; she looked completely absorbed in her new boyfriend, a rangy redheaded biology major with a pierced eyebrow I thought he would someday regret.

"How're you going to get back?" she asked. "You want the car, and you can pick me up tomorrow?"

I shrugged. "I may not be going back tonight. I'll find a way, don't worry."

We hugged, and I remember thinking how much I loved her. Neither of us jealous, both of us ready to watch each other's backs. When one of us had a guy around for a period of time, it was understood that the other one wouldn't be abandoned unless she was cool with going her own way. When things worked out the way it did the night I met Neil, both of us starting something new at the same time, it was perfect.

I could feel him looking at me as he waited by the door, leaning against the jamb with his hands shoved in his pockets. He had that birdlike tilt to his head, that considering, bemused expression. I loved how he was able to watch so steadily without trying to pretend he wasn't. I hadn't had more than one beer, but I slipped my arm through his as we headed out. That's how sure I was.

It turned out he didn't belong to that frat or any, to my relief. He, too, had been there to see a friend. He asked if I wanted to go out for food, or coffee, or he could make something at his place. I said his place, pretty much laying my cards out on the table, but he didn't change his manner any, didn't get too eager or start acting stupid because I was letting myself get picked up. We were on the same wavelength about the whole thing.

It was April in Cambridge at ten o'clock on a Friday night and it could have been cold or rainy. It could have even been snowing—raised in Boston, I wouldn't have been surprised.

It happened to be lovely. Warm weather had made studying hard for the last two weeks, and things were coming sooner than you were ready for them: magnolias, daffodils, even tulips had those hard green buds that were beginning to swell into color at the tips. The air was soft—inviting you to uncurl, let loose of that part you keep clenched against winter—and we talked all the way to his house, enough to know that we had plenty of ground to cover, that we weren't a couple of strangers who would run out of things to say after the first sex. We went up some back stairs that led directly into the kitchen of the house he shared. The plan was to do a stir-fry with tofu and vegetables. He was getting things out of the refrigerator, I was chopping celery, then he was beside me, rinsing vegetables at the sink, and I smelled the strong cumin scent of his sweat and felt the warmth coming off him in waves.

It was too hard. It was too hard to wait and do the normal things first, the washing, and chopping, and cooking, and eating. All I could feel was him standing there beside me, and he must have been feeling the same, how thick the current was between us. I couldn't even breathe right. I was afraid my hand would jerk and I would cut myself, so I put down the knife and stood there for a second, looking at my half-chopped stalk of celery, my little pile of pale green commas. Then he turned and put his face in my hair. His touch, what a relief it was, to be in the circle of his breathing, his smell, his arms.

There was no stopping, or slowing, it. For a day and a half we only left his bedroom when we had to eat, feeding ourselves with whatever we found in the kitchen, then going back to his mattress on the floor, locking his door, keeping his shades down. At one point he had to pull on his jeans and rifle through his housemate's stuff in the bathroom to find more condoms. By Sunday we were both sore, sticky, a little shaky.

I realized I'd never been in love before. I thought I had, all that kissing in cars and on beaches, all those late-night murmurings into the phone I had in my bedroom, trying not to wake up my mother, a light sleeper. I was conscious of our manless condition at home, the bare fact of my mother and me in the condo. At night, whispering into my phone to some boyfriend, I'd cup my palm around the reedy voice leaking back through the lit-up receiver with the same amount of guilt as if it were his semen I was somehow collecting, nowhere to put it among my mother's gifts to me: my hand-stitched Appalachian quilt, my Persian rug, my Stickley furniture.

It was a semen-free house, and always had been. Virginia, the

Virgin Prince, I nicknamed my mother maliciously and secretly in high school, when I went through that inevitable period of wanting to be an orphan, self-created and self-sufficient. It surprises me a little that I indulged in the same fantasy matricide as any other raging teenage girl, when I was already half an orphan by definition.

My anonymous father consists of a set of attributes my mother checked off at the donor bank. He was to be of reasonable height, with a high IQ and no known strains of mental illness. I asked her if he was also to be Caucasian, and she—feminist liberal Democrat— hedged, said something about the agency's policy of matching physical characteristics. I am certainly white. The whole Prince lineage is as white as it comes, descended from predominantly Dutch and English stock with a dash of German and Swiss.

But my father? Within a few parameters—white, sane, not a moron and not a dwarf—he could have been almost anyone. He must have been broke, to have sold his sperm. I've always imagined an impoverished hell-raiser, scaring up money for the down payment on a Mustang or a one-way ticket out of town. Of course he could have simply been a student scraping up tuition money, or a young husband trying to cover the mortgage and keep a roof over his *real* children, but that's not the way I like to think of him. I want to claim more recklessness from his genes, since on my mother's side everything came so precisely calibrated. The transaction that engendered me was a conventional arrangement, closed records and guaranteed anonymity for the donor, but I've recently heard of children writing letters through intermediate agencies to astonished midlife biological fathers; I've read about improbable reunions like these.

I prefer to let that person—whoever he is, not my father, certainly—be. I've had enough experience to know how meaningless an ejaculated burst of semen can be to a man. A spasm, a teaspoonful of fluid. And in the case of donor number whatever, in Boston in 1977, the afterglow included a check for some modest, but probably very welcome, sum.

There's a cartoon of a melodramatically drawn, career-suited woman clutching her head and saying, "Omigod—I forgot to have children!" That was not my mother. She prefers to cast herself as a victim of the patriarchy, claiming that men in her time were unwilling to marry a woman with ambitions equal to their own; men were intimidated by smart, highly educated women; men were not prepared to be true partners in the child-rearing enterprise. This is her way of saying she never found love.

Of course she loves me, and—despite our constant battling—I love her. But this was not a love she found, this was a love she *designed*. If you can understand that, you can understand Ginnie Prince. She expects to create her fate: mold it, refine it, and control it. Alone at thirty-nine, calculating the length of a gestation and weighing the odds of meeting, marrying, and conceiving with a suitable mate, she ordered me up.

She never seems to have regretted going it alone, but then my mother is not a wistful person. Right away, she expected the world to come around to her version of things. I didn't know Father's Day existed until fourth grade because my mother had blazed a trail ahead of me, meeting with preschool directors and school administrators, and insisting that all school-crafted cards and gifts earmarked for fathers be expunged from the scissors-and-paste curriculum to protect my feelings. Maybe they were sympathetic or maybe they were intimidated, but my mother, with her briefcase and half-glasses, every inch the Ivy League lawyer, would have left nothing to chance.

There's never been any man around in a consistent way except for Preston Baylor, my mother's legal partner and best friend since they met in a law school torts class where they were teamed up to work on a product liability brief. Preston has always been the nurturer. He's the one who kept markers and Jujubes in his desk for when I'd be marooned in the office on snow or fever days. He'd clear away his paperwork early and announce, I'm taking Julie for a hamburger, when my mother was still deep in her fourth conference call of the afternoon, filling pages of long yellow pads with scratched notes. She'd glance up, phone wedged between cheek and shoulder, and mouth, *Thank you*, without missing a beat of her scribbling.

No other man in her life, except for the occasional dinner date that always seemed to go well enough, even to the point of becoming a string of dinner dates, but never caught fire. Never became a situation where my mother and the man *had* to see each other, couldn't wait for the next opportunity to talk by phone or—God forbid—wake up next to each other. I'd ask her why not this one, why not that. But the architect had been fussy, she said, washing his hands too many times a day, keeping his white sneakers unnaturally spotless. She was bored to tears by the marathoner's zeal for timing wind sprints and calibrating micronutritional needs. And the journalist's travels had been unceasing, until he finally disappeared into a bureau in Malaysia, a vanishing spot on the horizon.

If she's been passionate about anybody, besides me and

Preston—who's gay, and taken besides—it would be her rafts of women friends. Get a clue, Julie—or *Emerald*—you might be thinking. Your mother is a lesbian.

I've made that mistake myself, first with the *aha* sense of having solved a mystery, then with a feeling of acceptance, and finally with a kind of impatience. *Get on with it, Mother,* was my attitude in college, *find yourself a nice girlfriend and admit it. Show some guts.*

If it's true, I'm convinced she doesn't know it herself. In one or two arguments we had when I was still at Wellesley, I tried to bait her with my discovery, get her to reveal some vulnerability, confusion—anything that would make me feel that she could possibly relate to my own unsettled state of mind. She just laughed it off, not defensively, but with the minor force of brushing aside an amusing misconception. It's possible that she's so massively repressed from her Boston Brahmin background that being gay is an idea she could never entertain. Or, the description just doesn't fit.

With little or no sexual experience, then, she's always claimed to know what my choices should be. She couldn't understand why, since my first crush on Timmy Wyatt in fourth grade, I've been drawn to underachieving boys, the ones who are extra big for their grades and make fun of everything behind the teachers' backs. We started having arguments about my friends early. I gave up expecting her to see what I saw, boys who didn't fit into an institutional groove and didn't want to, ones who defended themselves the only way they knew how, with humor and a smart mouth, and a talent for living in the moment.

If a boy told me he couldn't wait to get out of school—not to go to college but to drift, travel, find things out—I was interested. If he had a restless energy and a need for touch, I was excited. If he moved with an animal grace and his smile was subtle and his hunger became particular for me, I was most likely hooked.

High school was, by necessity, one long, elaborate deception. Oh, I took all the AP classes my counselors laid out for me. I was in school plays and on yearbook staff, and ran cross-country. But it was easy to create the record my mother demanded and live the life I was determined to. The teachers had no reason to scrutinize Ginnie Prince's signature as they read the notes excusing me for day trips, orthodontia appointments, pressing family obligations. My work didn't suffer, so they saw nothing to question about my frequent releases.

Once free, my friends and I had no real place to go. We'd drive to the beach and sit for hours, smoking cigarettes or dope and staring at the waves and imagining ourselves even more free— whatever that could mean. Somehow, even when skipping out on a honeyed October afternoon, we were irksomely accountable to adults. There must be a place, a way, we thought, to be under no one's thumb. To have the means to really decide our futures.

I went along with the whole Wellesley trip not because my mother was so set on it, but because I thought that finally our two agendas might actually intersect. She wanted me at her alma mater; I wanted to get out of our Back Bay condo. She could pay; I wanted some time and space to figure out my next move.

It worked out okay. I loved some of my classes—especially sculpting and pottery, especially getting my hands *into* something—and could pull off the grades my mother expected. I saw her just often enough to enjoy her wit and affection, but not so much that I felt pressured by the weight of her longings for me to be this perfect person she had in mind. Then I met Neil.

Those boys I'd known before were transformed now into car-toons—sweet, doe-eyed, comic in their simplicity. Neil touched something completely different in me as I lay in the crook of his arm, inhaling his spice. His gaze was focused above us as he talked about his work at M.I.T., how the thesis he'd been writing all year on the economics of deforestation was increasingly galling to him because it was just language, statistics, argument—while every day that he spent in the library acres of old-growth forest were being bulldozed and dozens of species were wiped out or endangered. I, in turn, was focused on his pale skin, the beauty of its pores and dark curling hairs. And the fact that I so miraculously cared, all of a sudden, not only about this body that I was drinking in, but about every word he said—his conviction a palpable, almost physical force, even when he was just talking, naked, on his back.

My mother is a great intellect, but her thinking is dispassion-ate. She has beliefs, even beliefs that are akin to Neil's, but her training as a lawyer has made her pragmatic. She talks about "real-world solutions" as if nothing in the real world deserves to be pure, whole, unfragmented. Until I met Neil, she pretty much had me convinced that life needed to be built out of compromise, Frost's "what to make of a diminished thing": a family out of two meager people, a settlement rather than a win or loss.

Neil, too, had been trying to do the "real-world" thing—go to a top school, get honors for his thesis, enroll in the Kennedy School in the fall, and then after that get a job in public policy. Find a cure within the system.

But every day, as part of his research, he was visiting websites that monitored direct action in the western forests: blockades of logging roads, equipment sabotage, lockdowns, cat and mouse with the loggers, and, most intriguing to him, tree-sits. He wanted to be there. He wanted the voles and the spotted owls and the ancient tree nicknamed "Grandma" to be real to him. He was jealous of the privations of activists suspended high in the air, fasting in their cargo nets when their ground resupply was cut off by law enforcement. He wanted to be there. He wanted to sleep in the canopy, be part of it. And that spring, as he worked on finishing his thesis, as I was earning my desultory scattering of A's and wondering how I could possibly spend another summer in my mother's condo or even our cottage on the Vineyard, he talked about it constantly. He whispered it in my ear as we made love—*how would you like to be fucked in the trees*—until the boutiques of Vineyard Haven or the air-conditioning of Marlborough Street started to seem like abominations, things utterly grotesque and unnatural. I began to want the forest the way I wanted Neil—its dampness, sharp smell, furred outline, protective arms and softly breathing dark. I felt our hungers merge into one hunger. I agreed to go.

3

My mother offered me France. Her friend Maura's ex-husband had bought a cottage in Provence and didn't want to hang around while the renovations were being made. You could invite Frida, she said. Live in the back part of the house, which isn't being worked on, and paint. You're always telling me you want to paint.

I had not mentioned painting for two years.

Then garden, if you're so interested in nature all of a sudden. The cottage has some very old grapevines, and an established herb garden. I wish someone would hand *me* a free summer in Provence to sketch and cook and read and grow things.

Why don't you go, Mother? Just go. Live in the cottage in Provence and put lavender in all your drawers. Bring along one of those cookbooks you keep buying. Make oxtail soup. Read the classics. Live the dream, Mom.

She offered me Paris, or a Eurail pass, or—more phone calls to friends, more pleas for help—a bed-sit in London that somebody's cousin was vacating for three weeks in July. If only I would not go to Oregon and live in a tree with Neil, who at that point had not yet found his name in the snake bends and coils of the river.

I hadn't myself talked about tree-sits with her. When I first brought up the trip, and Neil, I had stressed his research, the grade of distinction the committee had awarded his thesis. I had told her about the Economics of Deforestation and how important it was for him to see this at close range. I made sure she knew about the fellowship waiting for him at the Kennedy School, the job at the BLM or EPA or Interior that was sure to follow.

She ate this up, of course. She couldn't wait to meet him. The Friday night we were all going to have dinner I suggested he might wear the khakis and blue oxford shirt that hung clean and abandoned in the corner of his closet. The only actual clothes, in fact, *in* the closet. The working part of his wardrobe, the worn jeans and T-shirts and ancient flannel shirts that he *did* wear were always heaped on the floor, in various cycles of use and laundering. He gave me the backward tilted look, the amused squint around the eyes that meant he was trying to figure something out.

"I thought you didn't care what your mother thought."

"It's not that I *care* care. It's just a practical thing. Remove a layer of distraction so she can get to know you. Facilitate the interaction."

Neil said that if I wanted my mother to get to know him, he should wear what he usually wore. I pointed out that the Capital Grille was probably going to be full of guys in very nice suits.

My mother kept smiling when she saw us coming. I was hoping the darkness of the bar and all the heavy wood paneling would absorb the details of Neil's dress, that the faded flannel shirt—actually one of my favorites, soft as cattail fluff—would look "heathered" in an interesting *Men's Fashions of the Times* kind of way. I had dressed so as to draw the eye away from him and at the same time defy the stuffiness of the place in solidarity with him: black low-slung pants and a cropped black top that showed skin at the navel and a wide expanse of breastbone. I had put an exhausting amount of energy into that outfit, a depressing quantity of calculation and strategy. My silver and turquoise necklace, borrowed from Frida, was of the faux-hippie moment. My long hair was parted in the jagged, messy way that required many tries to get exactly right. I don't think Neil noticed how hard I had worked to diffuse his own, completely authentic messiness. But somehow it worked. My mother cocked one eyebrow slightly when we drew near, the right side of her mouth twitching slightly in a suppressed smile. I had created our "look," which somehow subsumed Neil's complete intolerance of convention and rendered us, at least in my mother's eyes in the dim light of the Capital Grille, at the cutting edge of youthful trendiness. It was another deception, of course.

I don't know why I bothered. We were still waiting to be served our meals when Neil's bluntness, his absolute inability to put a diplomatic spin on anything, began to lay the groundwork for what became my mother's total abhorrence of anything to do with him.

As soon as we had ordered drinks Ginnie began taking her deposition. She may have smiled, may have nodded and chuckled encouragingly, but she did that in trial, too. Nothing like a genuine conversation ever emerged when my mother was talking to one of my friends. She was incapable of letting the discussion follow its own path. There were areas she wanted to cover, and follow-up questions if the information wasn't forthcoming or specific enough. She needed to control everything, and did, because in these situations there was no opposing counsel to object to her leading, or to question the relevance of a particular line of probing.

"It isn't as though old-growth forest is a renewable resource," Neil was saying in response to my mother's assumption of the devil's advocate role. "Yes, you can replant and get these homogeneous, neatly managed forests. But when old growth is gone, it's gone. From any way you look at it, taking what's left of these areas is not the right way to produce lumber or sustain a region's logging economy. The price, for the ecosystem, for the national heritage, is just too great."

So far, so good. My mother, as I said, is a liberal and an environmentalist. But as Neil went on, warmed by his subject, by the first few swigs of his imported beer, by the expensive, cavelike atmosphere of the restaurant, my mother's gaze began to narrow and harden. It was one thing to feel strongly about the trees. Writing letters and signing petitions was good. Lobbying Congress was good. Getting a job within an institution of some power on the right side of the issue was good. But Neil began talking about how much he admired the activists. He enthused over strategies: spiking trees, pouring sugar or molasses into the engines of tree skidders, working at night to strew barbed wire and broken glass and drag fallen logs and branches across logging roads.

"It doesn't stop anything," he admitted. "But it slows them down. They lose whole days to restoring equipment and clearing roads. It adds costs to their operation and eats into the almighty bottom line."

"But under Clinton, wouldn't you say—"

"Under Clinton we've had empty promises. Flawed compromises. Maybe he's got the right impulses, but he's a politician above all, and he's hamstrung by a Republican Congress and by gridlock with labor interests. He wants to give a piece of cake to everybody, and as a result, we've got legislation like the disastrous timber salvage rider he signed with a budget bill in 1995 because the Republicans held his feet to the fire on appropriations. In a single stroke Clinton—our best hope in a long time—opened up roadless and fragile riparian areas to logging trucks. Prohibited appeals of salvage sales. Overrode existing injunctions."

My mother arched her eyebrows and held her hands up in mock surrender. "Realpolitik is never very satisfying to idealists," she said wryly. "But back to the activists and their methods." She smiled falsely, taking a sip of her martini. "Surely, you, yourself, wouldn't want to do anything illegal. Not with your bright future." She conferred her most approving look on him, on his M.I.T. credentials and Kennedy School prospects, on his thesis grade of distinction and potential to perform honest, legitimate work for the civic good. Perhaps she was thinking of his possible political future; she herself had once run for and lost the election to a seat in the state legislature. She had blamed herself for not working hard enough, not meeting enough people, which I took as subtle regret for my very existence. I was in seventh grade at the time, hated making small talk with strangers, and balked at going to her candidate coffees. She went without me to two or three a week, but stopped short of the nonstop whirl she would have plunged herself into had she not been saddled with an awkward, antisocial twelve-year-old. Not that those ambitions in her had been vanquished: Preston had recently told me that she had put herself forward for a judgeship and that the political wheels of appointment were grinding forward.

"You bet your—" We all heard the ghostly *ass* Neil just managed to swallow, and in the half-beat pause I managed to flash on my mother's still-trim, cellulite-free ass, how she kept it tight by training for a half marathon once a year, how she loved to offer it to the sun, lying on her stomach in an athletic two-piece, sunbathing in a post-skin-cancer world her one reckless gesture.

"You bet I would. After all the legislation I've analyzed, the political posturing that turns out to be worth nothing in the end except some pro-environment rhetoric in someone's campaign speech—"

"But you have so much to offer. Shouldn't you be one of the leaders, the thinkers? Even if I grant you—and I don't, by the way —but even if, for the sake of the argument, I agree that there have to be some foot soldiers in the effort, some people to agitate and get attention—"

"It's not about getting attention. It's not about any one person."

"All right. But still. Don't you owe it to the whole movement to use your intellectual capital wisely?" My mother flashed her winning-over smile, the one that got witnesses for the opposing side to lose their head and trust her, the surprising *warmth* of it. "You're obviously too good to throw away on some petty arrest for chaining yourself to a truck. Don't you think you bear your talents at least that much responsibility?"

Neil never flattered me or anyone. He called his professors by their first names whether they asked him to or not. His attitude about wealth and privilege was that if it offered you a good meal and a good beer in a well-upholstered restaurant you should enjoy your dinner, but it didn't mean you owed anyone anything. My mother couldn't have known how deeply her rhetoric urging him to join the elite would offend him.

"I don't think I'm better than anyone," he said quietly, breaking eye contact with her for the first time. At that moment I sensed he was writing her off, and that any overtures she henceforth offered would be wasted. I had no evidence for this beyond a sudden intuition he could do this: see people as either worthy of him or not, and that once he had judged them undeserving, there would be no second chances.

"Well, my goodness, I don't think it's a question of being *better*," my mother said, looking at me with an expression of baffled helplessness. "Not in the sense of claiming more for yourself. Not in that class way. But *gifts*. That's what I'm talking about—God-given talents. Surely you must admit they come with some. . . ." Here she cast her eyes about the rich paneling, hunting for a synonym. My mother loved to be thought of as eloquent, and would not have liked to use the word *responsibility* redundantly. Mentally I supplied her from our Yankee word hoard—*burdens, duties, accountabilities*—but our telepathy failed and she drew a blank. "Julie, you know what I'm saying. Don't you agree?"

Neil had no history with Ginnie Prince. He could hear her silken "Don't you agree?" and not be thrown back to a million arguments he'd had with her over everything from the correct age to start wearing pantyhose to whether teenage girls had a right to visit their gynecologists alone. He probably didn't hear the coerciveness I heard in those words, the presumption that thoughts obeyed twists of the double helix, so it would naturally follow that I would feel, see, and think like my mother since I sprang from her womb (never mind my wild card father, my trump, my *out*). I hated the fake flattery of my mother's *Don't you agree?*, the way the words had promoted me at age nine to a mini-adult so I could engage in a mock debate with her—very mock, extremely mock, since there was to be no question as to whose vision would triumph. (How different my mother's *Don't you agree?* was from Preston's *What do you think?*)

Neil just chewed. Simply finished his bite of salmon and reached for another slice of bread and said coolly—no history with her, no churning resentments—"Spin it all you like, Virginia, but you're talking about the privileges of a meritocracy, and I'm talking about what we each owe to the planet itself. Doesn't matter if you're a Kennedy or some farm boy. Doesn't matter if you're covered in degrees or if you're a high school dropout. Education doesn't matter. What matters is conviction. And action, real action that makes news and strikes directly at the heart of the economic monoliths. All the rest"—he waved a hand airily—"is just words."

I'd been in the process of trying to frame a reply to my mother, trying to say something that I really thought, not what either she or Neil would have me say, when Neil had overridden my silence. I was registering this with the slightest irritation when it was superseded by pleasure at hearing him address my mother, uninvited, by her first name. If he had called her "Ms. Prince," she would have immediately asked him to call her "Ginnie," granting him the favor of that intimacy. But instead he had decided himself what to call her, adult to adult. I was sure she was too piqued now to offer "Ginnie." Virginia it would be. Frosty, formal, the declaration of their adversarial status.

My mother laughed, a small mirthless sound. "If you really think that barbed wire on roads and—what did you say?—spikes in trees constitute a strike 'at the heart of economic monoliths'—"

Neil buttered his bread evenly. "Millions of dollars in lost time, equipment, and manpower. Ten times more than the slap-on-the-wrist fines the courts pass out."

She looked at him, her powerful gifts of pretense, the ability to smile through anything, beginning to desert her. When she turned to me, the smoothness, the control, were gone. I recognized panic in her, something I'd seen only a few times—when I was eight and the passing driver had knocked me off my bike, the time I'd stayed out all night my senior year.

"Julie, you're not going to be part of this? Sweetie, think about what you're getting involved in. This is serious, illegal stuff. Jules, please."

I refused to meet her pleading eyes. To tell the truth, when I'd told Neil I'd go, I wasn't thinking about the work. I was thinking about the trees, about being fucked in the trees, about running away with him. I was picturing our cross-country trip in his van, how cozy we'd make it with blankets and pillows, how we'd stop wherever we wanted to swim, or eat, or doze in each other's arms.

I felt him watching me, but I didn't look up to see if it was his smiling, knowing expression, or if he was trying to telegraph something like *Say what you need to say*, or *I want to be with you no matter what.*

I felt stretched between their looks. My mother's, who wasted her love on no one but me. Neil's, who kept his distance from the word *love*, but held me so tightly in the dark sometimes that I could scarcely breathe.

"I'm going, Mother," I said, lifting my chin. "It's going to be fine. I won't get into any trouble. Don't worry."

"Don't tell me not to worry." Her earrings flashed as they bobbed. "The whole thing is lunacy. It's absurdly, pointlessly self-destructive. If it would do any good I'd simply forbid you to go, but that hasn't worked for a long time." She grew still and fixed a rueful gaze on me. I felt for a second that Neil wasn't present at the table, that my mother and I were wrapped in a bubble of our own history that sealed everyone else out. To break it, I turned to him.

"You don't *want* to get arrested, do you, Neil? I mean, that's not the goal, is it?"

"Of course not. I want to contribute, do some work that matters." He bumped my knee under the table and pressed it there. Maybe then he was thinking what I was, about finding swimming holes and hot springs where we would strip naked and be nowhere except joined to each other. I pressed back.

Somehow we all made it through the rest of the dinner. Somehow I lasted through the ensuing days of my mother's campaign to send me in any direction but to the forests. When I kissed her goodbye a week and a half later, she pressed a new cell phone into my hand, and an envelope.

"I mean for this money to be yours. Not his, not even both of yours. *Yours*. Save it for an emergency. Keep it in a safe place."

"All right," I said.

"Call me, please. Don't make me wonder where you are."

"All right."

Then she held me to her as if she might never see me again. Neil was double-parked below on Marlborough Street. My mother and I embraced in the marble foyer with the half-moon table where I used to throw my backpack after school. The zippers will scratch the finish, Julie, my mother had said a couple of thousand times. Then why the hell is there a table there? I would retort. Don't be fresh, she'd say. And on it would go, neither of us changing our parts. The zippers *had* damaged the table. Fine scratches like you'd get from plunging bare arms into a rosebush. I had done that. I was sorry now.

4

I gave my mother her money's worth at first. I loved the cell phone, the way it folded up and slid, a compact weight, into the pocket of my overalls, the way the word *roaming* appeared tiny at the top of the screen whenever I called her. If Neil and I had done nothing but *roam* all summer, satisfying oddball curiosities and spur-of-the-moment whims, I might still be pretty much the same Julie. Sheer totals of miles on the odometer wouldn't have changed me.

Neil was torn between his desire to get there, to not miss anything, and his wish, like mine, to enjoy ourselves. We hurried and we dallied. He'd take huge bites of interstate, and then, sick like me of the sameness, of the greasy fast food, he'd listen to one of my suggestions from the AAA guidebook. A blues club in Chicago. A lake campground off the beaten path in Wisconsin. A Native American museum in South Dakota. He used my phone a couple times to check in with people he'd been in contact with. Every time he talked to one of them he'd hang up slightly distracted, a little less present. I began to feel jealous of them, those pure believers he couldn't wait to join, the high-minded ones. I tried to tell myself that after working for a year in the abstract, with only language and numbers to keep him company, it was natural that he'd want to see the forests he'd written about. It wasn't that I wasn't real to him. It was that he needed a year's worth of imaginings to be real, too.

I was growing used to the difference in the way Neil and I perceived things. In Cody, I fell right in to the spirit of the cowboy kitsch. I made Neil stop so that we could look in the gift shops, where I felt his boredom weighing at my side like a too-heavy shoulder bag. I couldn't help myself. I bought a silver ring with a round turquoise stone and a little beaded medicine bag that hung on a string around my neck.

"That turquoise probably isn't even from around here," Neil chided as I paid for my purchases. "Isn't that supposed to be a New Mexico thing?"

I didn't care that he couldn't see the point. The ring was beautiful, simple and smooth, and symbolized for me the West. And who knew what I might collect for the medicine bag? What seeds or stones or charms?

I loved Cody—its split logs and squat western facades, its galleries and shearlings and street signs reading HEART MOUNTAIN STREET and STAMPEDE AVE. I couldn't persuade Neil to pull into Trail Town to see the cluster of settler cabins and the grave site of "Liver Eating" Johnson, or to stop at the Historical Center with the colorful tipis pitched out front next to the flagpole. He snorted when I told him the admission price from the visitor's magazine I'd picked up. We did have cheeseburgers at the Irma, the hotel Buffalo Bill built and named after his daughter, and once again I wished we were just on vacation, like other couples drinking beer out of bottles marked with colorful microbrewery labels I couldn't quite make out in the restaurant's shuttered afternoon dark.

Neil was even more conscious of money by now, which made me more conscious of not having to worry about it, with my Visa card whose bill Preston would pay for me out of my trust fund account, courtesy of my late Grandfather Prince. When I'd turned twenty the summer before, a portion of my funds had come available, and for the first time I didn't have to ask my mother for money. It had changed the whole balance of our argument the weeks before I left; we both knew she couldn't forbid me to go, and I'd wondered, not for the first time, if Grandfather Prince had quite realized what he was doing, if he'd intended to curtail my mother's authority over me. As far as I could tell, they'd been friendly, if not demonstrative, allies, subscribing to similar theories of life: Work hard, achieve much, assume your natural station as a leader. If they'd had disagreements about how I should be raised, or even if I should have come into the world in the first place, they'd kept them hidden from me. My trust fund was to mature in three stages, the final installment when I reached thirty-five, in keeping with Grandfather Prince's philosophy of providing seed money to support education and travel, or perhaps a period of volunteer service or internship, while not making me so rich as a college student that I wouldn't have to choose a profession. It had worked for Ginnie, maybe it would for me as well.

All I was certain of at the moment was that the burden of accountability had been lifted, and that my mother knew it, too. My situation couldn't have been more different from Neil's, who, though he'd been on scholarship as a student, had only a meager stake for the trip, scraped up from the refunded deposit on his room and the fact that he'd prepaid his last month's rent.

I would have gladly paid for that lunch and a dozen others, but Neil's voice had gotten snappish when I'd offered to treat in the beginning, so I'd stopped asking. To get around the fact that I was charging most things and Neil was paying cash, he would count out and pay me his share. If I'd been a different kind of girl, more comfortable with her wealth, or less careful with Neil's pride, I'd have put a stop to those awkward transactions. *For Christ's sake, I don't want your money,* that girl would have said with an irritated tone that brooked no argument. He would have given in with silent ill grace and would have never offered to pay again. *That's* what I didn't want—the sexual chemistry to tip—and I knew it would happen if I started playing the heiress.

As we drove west from Cody, outcroppings of rock began to define the flat, buff-colored ranchland below. Gradually stone walls rose, sharp and striated, making me feel like I was passing through a portal. I caught myself holding my breath as the landscape changed, thinking, *Everything is about to be different.* It wasn't that I was an inexperienced traveler—my mother had first taken me to Paris when I was six. By high school I'd seen most of the European capitals, as well as most major U.S. cities. New York was almost as familiar to me as Boston. I'd been to

Barbados, Puerto Rico, St. Kitts, and Jamaica. When we were about to go somewhere new my mother would get me books about the place from the library. Before visiting foreign countries we'd see odd, subtitled movies. Ginnie prided herself on her worldly child who, for math problems on the plane, performed currency conversions and could greet people in four languages.

So it came as a surprise to me, as we climbed and the stone began forming itself into towers and ridges, a skein of river unwinding to our left, the cattle thinning on the shrinking grasslands, how disoriented it all made me feel. Paradoxically, I felt a rush of homecoming at the same time I was registering its strangeness. *So this is how it is,* I thought. Like going back to a place half dreamed or half remembered.

Then the forest rose up out of the stone. First a few trees dotting the rocky slopes, then a bunch of trees shouldering together, and then, without being able to pinpoint exactly when it happened, we were suddenly enfolded in shadowy green. The sky wasn't just everywhere anymore, in the slatternly way of the Plains states. It was something rarer, intricate and shaped, meeting the trees at their tips.

Neil perked up when we entered the east Yellowstone gate. He'd been here before, as a kid with his parents, and there was something now of the eight-year-old glowing in his face as we scanned the woods on either side of us for animals. His family had camped, he told me, he and his sister nestled in sleeping bags, bookended by their parents. At night he'd had difficulty dropping off to sleep not because he was frightened of the noises outside the tent, but because he wanted to hear them all—hoped that a bear would come sniffing after the leftover cooking smells hovering around their embers. They'd taken weeks, what seemed like an enormous span to a child, to drive there from Massachusetts and take their time seeing the park, migrating from geysers to canyons to lake country. It was the best time, Neil said, he'd ever spent with his family. I could understand that the trip was a high point, but there was something more to his tone, a note of sourness that deflected further discussion. It was always like that when I asked him about his family, some subtext of disappointment in his reply that he'd never care to elaborate on. Rather than press him now, I let him enthuse, both of us enjoying his recollections of a time that seemed uncomplicated by any resentments. When the trees thinned and we got our first glimpse of the lake, he breathed a soft "There it is," as if coming upon its extraordinary blue were a retrieval of something he owned but had misplaced.

Before this trip with Neil, I'd never camped, not really. The closest I'd come was two weeks in the Berkshires, bunking in a whitewashed cabin with my childhood friend Sara and some other girls who remain indistinct in memory, all of us supervised by a skinny counselor with a single braid down her back and an overbite. I don't recall having had any profoundly moving encounters with nature there; in fact we tried to talk the counselors out of taking us on trail hikes whenever we could. We were lazy with adolescence; like lionesses, we needed to spend large portions of the day sunning in groups. I do remember the extravagant darkness of the place at night, the way the stars seemed fake in their outrageous numbers, and the way I never seemed to look in a mirror there—maybe there weren't any—though when I finally did return to my reflection at home in my bedroom, I was shocked to see I'd somehow been made starkly beautiful by the fresh air and lake water and sun.

Ginnie later heard something she didn't like about the place— a counselor from another cabin got busted for pot—and I never went back. My other camps were urban sojourns, in keeping with the rest of my life: once taking the T daily to ballet camp in the South End, another time staying at a nearby college for two weeks of gymnastics camp. There was art camp at the Museum School, drama camp at the Y. I was a city kid, except for our summer weeks on the Vineyard, where I sometimes did as much shopping and eating out as I did in Boston.

We set up camp near Bridge Bay and took showers. I volunteered to sit with our laundry while it agitated in the aluminum drums and then I wondered why I did. I was always doing that— tidying up the campsite, collecting the litter from the van. I tried to tell myself it was just a personality difference, not a gender thing. Neil just didn't see the point of certain types of order, especially when they were so temporary and hard to maintain. I, on the other hand, felt best when everything was where it belonged. I didn't think I was freakish about it or anything—Frida and I had never seemed out of sync—but sharing space with Neil seemed to bring out a certain obsessiveness in me, maybe because his method of letting everything fall where it would seemed like such a disturbing kind of entropy. My mother and I had had a pair of housecleaners descend on us every other week—a married Portuguese couple who exchanged volleys of cross words with each other as they stormed through our condo with military efficiency. I'm sure they regarded us as an easy job, nothing out of place and nothing to pick up, just the wholly forgivable residue of two weeks' occupancy—a light patina of dust; a little soap scum gathered around the drains. My mother hadn't needed to scold me into being neat; I just naturally fell into certain habits. I guess before I started looking for ways to be different from her I was looking for ways to be like her. One of my favorite pastimes as a child was taking all the toys and books off my shelves and putting them back in groupings that were the most pleasing to the eye.

I had brought a book to read while the laundry finished but found myself daydreaming instead on the plastic molded chair, feet drawn up so that my chin rested on my knees. Rows of washers rocked and dryers flumphed. The park village was a cozy island of domesticity. In the campground older couples walked dogs, and children played tag. Families came back from trips to the marina store loaded down with grocery bags, and in front of me a man was folding his clean clothes on a table. I liked the comfort and familiarity of it. It was like playing house when there was no actual house to be bound by. If I were honest, I'd have had to admit that I was trying it out. I didn't intend to be alone at my mother's age, though she'd succeeded in making me assume I wouldn't marry for years to come. But Neil's presence day and night, his smell, his smile, his voice—they were growing into my very consciousness, making me wonder if this was what marriage was like, the boundaries between us so blurry. Even this brief separation to do the laundry felt like a mild shock, a type of exposure.

Thinking about him gave me enough energy to get up, stretch, and open the dryer door to check our stuff. As I folded it (some of the waistbands still damp, but I was suddenly impatient) I tried not to indulge in making pointless perfect angles to the bends of the shirtsleeves. Neil, after all, would simply stuff his shirts into the bag, so why did it matter to me? Somehow it did, but I tried to temper it, didn't try for perfect symmetry with my own shorts and T-shirts, either.

I found him napping in the tent. "Are you ready to go on that walk?" I asked him, snuggling into his side.

"Mmmh," he sighed, pulling me into his hollows until we had our perfect jigsaw fit.

"It'll be dark soon," I reminded him.

For an answer he just nuzzled my hair, and then I gave in, too, to the delicious comfort of it, floating in our private peace, the raft that held us, for the moment, completely free of want or outside pressures. It felt sinful to be so satisfied, but no, that wasn't quite the word. Not sin, but luck.

5

udman was our contact. He'd told Neil to leave our van at a member's house in Eugene and catch a ride with a guy named Shaman who shuttled people to the site. The dashboard of Shaman's battered Toyota was adorned with numerous artifacts from Other Places, beads and carved figures and little woven purses that seemed to bulge with talismans. Neil tried to make conversation during the ride, but Shaman's replies were short and oblique and left no place for any exchange. He scared me. He offered no information and seemed to want none, telling us by his indifference he was only our usher. Usher to where, I suddenly, flutteringly, didn't know: To the edge of something? A place where who we were or where we had come from didn't matter? From the back seat I compared Shaman's graying braid tied up with a buckskin lace and Neil's thick dark hair, just washed in the shower at the last motel we allowed ourselves. I wondered again if Neil knew what he was getting us into, if he cared.

Our route led us on a succession of shrinking roads, as if we were traveling down a rabbit hole in Wonderland. We spent only minutes on the interstate before exiting to a two-lane state highway bordered by pastures. Then we turned at a covered bridge, not to drive across it, but beside it, over a newer bridge. The covered bridge itself sat fenced off like a museum piece beyond the guardrail. I wanted to stop and walk through its shade, feel its ghosts, but was too intimidated by Shaman's silence to ask. A couple of lean men in jeans and billed caps fished off the road into the reservoir. Past the reservoir the road proceeded through a small town named Lowell, whose sign told us it sat at an elevation of seven thousand feet, with a population of just over a thousand. Another Massachusetts doubling: first a Springfield, then a Lowell. Probably coincidence, since those names were common enough, but I'd read in my Oregon guidebook that the founders of Portland had flipped a coin over whether to name it Boston or Portland, after each man's hometown in New England, and I'd wondered: Why would you go all that way just to remind yourself of what you left? Why wouldn't you look around for a brand-new word for it?

We drove past a high school, a row of tackling dummies lined up across the field, then turned again at an intersection marked by another unused covered bridge, another relic—though I saw from the sign that its date was 1936, hardly antique by Massachusetts standards. I wanted to joke to Neil that back home the bridges were old and the trees were young, and out here it was just the opposite, but I filed that comment away with all the other casual chat I didn't feel comfortable making in Shaman's presence. It was a beautiful afternoon in June, but we encountered practically no one, met no traffic, saw only a man in overalls who didn't look up from sprinkling grains of something, fertilizer or seed, onto a patch of his property. The land stretched into pasture again, but with a backdrop of close hills rising up, the forests close enough to reach out to now. A brown colt with white stockings broke into a canter, running for a few moments with us on its side of the split-rail fence, and I thought of Sara and her pampered horse Little, also a bay with white stockings. All the hours spent grooming and tending her as if she were our child, ten times our size.

At a seam marked by a cattle guard crossing, our country road suddenly transformed into a USFS number and shrank some more, into two tiny doll-sized lanes. As it began rising up out of the farmland into the first level of trees, the yellow line dividing it vanished and the asphalt nipped in again to just the width of a single car, with scalloped turnouts on the bends and blind hills. A thin stream emerged from the trees on our right; it stayed twinned to our road in sinuous rising bends. Now and again there were signs for recreation areas pointing off to small roads and parking lots, and in between we came upon an occasional car parked at a precarious tilt on the shoulder, its inhabitants nowhere to be seen. The creek stayed with us like a faithful pet, and once I caught a glimpse of a man and a boy sitting side by side on rocks, motionless with fishing poles. After a final sign pointing off to a campground—PROTECT AND ENJOY YOUR FOREST—the stream turned decisively away from us at the same moment the pavement abruptly changed to gravel. I was having trouble imagining logging trucks negotiating this tiny twisting road, increasingly rutted with deep holes, and I asked Shaman if they really could. He replied that they could and did. His shortness seemed more rude than frightening to me now; my intimidation was ebbing, and his tone irritated me into further asking what the yellow shrubby flowers were—gorse?

"Scotch broom."

At which point I gave up trying to talk to Shaman.

We were passing under arches of moss-draped branches that dimmed the sunlight, though it still sliced in irregularly through the boughs. I was paging through the inch-square photographs of conifers and pines in my Audubon guide, trying to sort out the Douglas Firs. The Western Red Cedars were easy with their stripy, fibrous bark. Were all the rest Douglas Firs? I wasn't about to ask Shaman anything else, figuring Neil would know and tell me when we were out of the car; thinking it was also a tad ridiculous to be seen as someone charging in to save trees you couldn't even recognize.

After miles of bumping along on the gravel, one rut jarring the Toyota so badly I thought an axle must have snapped, Shaman pulled over at what, to me, was a point indistinguishable from stretches of road before it. He parked on the narrow turnout.

"Just follow this line here." He traced his blunt index finger on the hand-drawn, xeroxed map. "It's about half a mile to the camp, due west. You shouldn't have any problem. Trail's decent."

I peered over Neil's shoulder and saw little drawings of boulders, an arrow pointing to a log over a creek, some drawings of trees marked *Big Brothers* at a fork.

"What's that?" I asked, pointing.

"Couple of massive Doug Firs side by side. Course there's lots of 'em, but those ones are huge. Can't miss 'em if you're on the trail."

And if we're not? And by the way, which ones are the "Doug" Firs? But Shaman and Neil were all business, getting our packs out of the trunk. At the motel I'd sorted what to take with me and what to leave stored in the van. Bring layers, Mudman had advised in a previous e-mail. I had those, several changes of underwear and socks, some eco-friendly toothpaste and a toothbrush. A hairbrush. We didn't know how long we'd be in the woods, but Mudman said plan for ten days or so. My compact of birth control pills didn't take up much room, but then I'd realized that my cycle was due to end and I'd need a box of tampons. Instead, I decided to try a trick that Frida had told me about, starting the next pill cycle right up without the week of placebos in between. I wasn't thrilled about messing with my body this way, engineering it to skip a period entirely, but if I was already tricking it into not ovulating, I didn't see how this could be any worse. I hadn't been keen on starting the pills in the first place, but the methods we'd been using seemed less viable in the woods. Leave no trace, right? I didn't want our latex condoms to be buried out there forever, and I didn't want to put them in with any group garbage, or save them and pack them out myself.

Mudman had given us a shopping list to fill, and even though Neil was carrying the heavier load, my straps dug uncomfortably into my shoulders when I put the pack on. Everything he'd ordered was dense: lentils, miso powder, beans, peanut butter, powdered milk, batteries. But it felt good to be coming with a contribution. Neil hadn't protested when I'd offered to pay this time. Charity for the cause, not him.

Shaman said so long, and we watched him maneuver his car back and forth in the tiny turnout until he faced the opposite way. Then, without waving, he drove off, gravel crunching under him.

Silence. A crow caw. Then silence again.

"Whoa," Neil said. "Isn't this great?"

We were standing in some long grass that merged into forest a few feet away—no one at all to witness our departure. Like a fairy tale, I thought. Just push into the dark woods until you discover the strangers living there. Stay until you've gotten what you came for, then make the journey back. Or not, I thought with a sudden twist of fear: Hansel and Gretel—did some gentle woodsman eventually bail them out? I couldn't remember.

"Look at the little piles of rocks," Neil said. When we looked down, we could see the subtle arrangements someone had made to guide us—stones, a pointing stick, a dotted line of bark pieces.

"What if we get lost?"

"We won't."

I followed him, my eyes down the whole time, trying to follow the anonymous messages. It got easier, and then I'd relax, and then I'd lose track of the signs, and then I'd have a few seconds' panic until I saw another. In Yellowstone the rangers had tied gay little plastic ribbons around tree trunks or sprayed color-coded arrows when they were marking backwoods trails. It began to sink in that we were joining an underground movement, that this trail wasn't meant to be followed by just anyone, that the forest we were walking through was contested ground, each tree like a child in a custody battle.

After a while I heard creek sounds that soon materialized into the creek itself, a mere thread of the stream we'd driven along-

side before, but still a friendly burble over rocks and some mossy logs.

"Our bridge, m'lady," Neil said, offering me his hand to walk across the log. It wasn't the kind of gesture he made often, holding a hand out to help me, so maybe he was sensing my nervousness. Past the stream our path seemed to curve, though I was spending more time futilely hunting for the piles of stones and branches than I was seeming to find them. That branch lying on the ground—was it pointing or not? Then Neil stopped dead in front of me, frowning.

"Do you think we lost it?" My heart started to hammer.

"No, no." But there he was tracing his finger over the line and looking back over his shoulder in little glances. I looked, too, and saw only trees closing around us in undifferentiated forest. What fucking trail?

My phone was fully charged but turned off. Out here there would be no way to charge it again once I'd used up the power. And then again, maybe we wouldn't even get a signal if I tried; in Yellowstone I'd gotten only the little icon of the phone with a cancel sign over it, as if to say, *You roamed too far, sweetie.*

Neil kept searching the paper as if he'd missed some subtlety in the kindergarten-style drawing. He shouldn't have curved after the stream, I thought, angry with both him and myself. I had *known* we weren't seeing markers. Why hadn't I spoken up? Why did I just cede authority to him? He wasn't automatically better at this Indian scout stuff than I was.

I closed my eyes and tried to exhale a calming breath, then gave my shoulders a few rolls to relieve them of the weight, which was beginning to hurt. Could we find the road again if we had to? All we'd have to do was let ourselves be pulled downhill, gravity leading us back down the mountain to the gravel, which would return us eventually to the reassuring asphalt, and some neighborly people with RVs we were sure to find clustered at the campground.

We retraced our steps to the stream, then picked our way through what seemed the straighter path.

"Up there." I pointed. "Do you think they're the Big Brothers?"

Neil consulted his map, his compass, the potential twin gray pillars we were seeing through the maze of trees. "Let's go see," he said. "I think we're still off the trail now, anyway."

You just said we were not *off the trail,* I wanted to say. *You just lied to me.* Except that as we grew nearer and saw that the trees ahead were indeed massive, the trunks deeply furrowed like elephant hide, I began to forgive him. I had found them. We stood in front of them, unable to resist spending several moments just looking straight up to where the lowest branches began, at the height where other trees reached their pinnacle. I thought how we were a funny inverse of rubes in the big city walking around with heads tilted back to take in the skyscrapers. Douglas Fir, I taught myself, memorizing the pattern of the ridged bark and palette of brown to gray with reddish hints.

I felt more confident as we walked on, more trusting of our joint abilities to figure things out, work through a situation. He wasn't trying to take over, but if I let him, then he had no choice, right? It was up to me to stay a real person here, a grown-up and not his dependent. Those sudden surges of anger that flared in me now and then, were they really about him? I recognized them too well. *All you have to do is not disappear,* I told myself. *You're not his little girl and you're not Ginnie's. The days when she controlled everything about you—the color of your room, your choice of friends, the lessons you had to take after school—are over. You wouldn't be here at all if she was still running your life, remember?*

And where was here, exactly? It was damp and gloomy, and I had to keep my eyes out to avoid squishing the moss-colored slugs in front of me when I wasn't scrutinizing the side of the trail for markers. I shivered despite the layers I wore—camisole, T-shirt, sweatshirt. I *didn't* know where. More to the point, I didn't know *why*. My mother's arguments against this whole enterprise echoed in my ears. Absurd. Pointless. Self-destructive. The trees themselves weren't helping; they loomed uncomfortably above me, and they were a sinister green, almost black, prematurely darkening the afternoon. They were just trees, and they seemed to be doing all right without Neil and me, and there were an awful goddamn lot of them.

I almost bumped into Neil when he stopped in front of me. He reached back and grabbed my arm in a gesture that made me stay quiet.

A doe and fawn crossed about fifteen feet in front of us, then froze as we had. The mother locked her liquid eyes with ours, while the twiglike baby at her flank seemed to disappear into their joint stillness.

The best part was, she didn't bolt. After holding us for a few seconds—during which I think I saw Neil nod to her as if to say, *Go ahead, it's yours*—she regally turned and walked on, the fawn picking its way behind. We let them get fully out of sight, the trees folding around them, before we moved. Neil turned and gave me a little smile and I liked that he didn't say a word. We kept our part of the silence around us, and when we went forward into the space the deer had emptied, I imagined I was stepping into her neutral calm, her peace. And so began my bargain with the woods.

6

They looked up at the first sound of us snapping through the woods, then two of them came forward to greet us. Mudman was lean and blond in a way I hadn't pictured, like a Norwegian schoolboy, his wrists hanging out of his sweater sleeves. Starling looked sturdy and thick next to him, her brown hair pulled back into a ponytail, her body obscured under men's overalls. When Neil had told me about the aliases, I'd assumed that the names the owners chose would fit them better than any that parents could give to blank newborns. But the more people I got to know in the movement, the more I realized that the self-naming was a kind of wishing. Starling, with her solid legs and torso, seemed to wish for delicacy. Mudman's choice puzzled me, though I did come to note a certain fastidiousness in the way he organized us. Maybe he wanted his name to downplay his orderly nature, or maybe he named himself after the mud because it preoccupied him—he felt dirty, and what he wanted was to be clean.

I couldn't remember all the names at first, I was so distracted by the images they produced, as if I'd been invited to a piece of performance art and had to figure out relationships between the code words and faces. I almost made the mistake of laughing when introduced to Spiderman, but something stopped me. He, of all of them, demanded to be taken seriously. I later found out he was the one who volunteered for the most dangerous climbs, and who took the lead in setting the initial rigging. The risks he seemed to seek verged on suicidal, and it was something in his eye, a kind of hostile defiance and come-on at the same time, that warned me not to treat his name like a joke.

Neil and I were told to give only our movement names. I felt Starling's reserve even as she showed us around: the underground spring, the refuse pit, the compost-crappers, the wood stash, and the "warren," a lean-to shelter made out of fallen branches and camouflaged tarp. No one wanted to know how far we had come or how long we would stay. It was like walking in on a party and the only thing that mattered to the other guests was who you were about to be among them. Here is the game, here are the rules, let's see you play.

The first rule was to take an action. It wasn't until Neil and I scrambled through the woods with Starling the next morning to bring supplies to the sitters that I felt we began to count. We had told our names over breakfast—oatmeal and tea made on a cookstove—and I had felt immediately stupid over mine, inane and girlish. Neil's "River" sounded right, but I wanted to grab my new name back and say, *Wait—I made a mistake, it's all wrong, I'm sorry,* but of course that would have made everything worse, so I let the unfortunate "Emerald" hang in the air. I had reached after some notion of beauty and ended up with only the embarrassing evidence of my self-romanticizing. My face grew hot and I looked down, but not before I saw Starling and others smile back encouragingly, and Spiderman smirk under his mustache.

We followed Starling as she made her way through the woods according to some internal sense of direction. She and Mudman, a couple, I began to understand, had been here awhile—"long enough" was all they would say, their evasiveness a casual rebuke for asking inappropriately specific questions—and they were as at home in the forest as if it were a suburban backyard. Most of the forest people were around my age (though one boy—Brave— looked so young I'd figured him to be a runaway, someone who stumbled into the woods rather than hitting the streets of Portland or Seattle), but Starling and Mudman were probably closer to Neil's age, and I wondered if they'd spent most of their twenties doing this. She was explaining that there were two trees rigged at the moment, both with platforms. The sitters could traverse the lines from one tree to another and visit each other when there wasn't any activity. The action now was two-pronged. A mile away, the movement was making sporadic assaults on the loggers' equipment as an access road was being bulldozed to the new cutting area. Meanwhile, these oldest, or at least biggest, firs in the cutting zone had been set up for occupancy. As we walked, Starling pointed out a flash of orange paint on the bark of a couple of trees we passed.

"Marked for saving. Supposedly," she said.

"Part of the fifteen percent hold-back?" Neil asked.

Starling snorted. "What they do," she said, "is make the sale fifteen percent bigger, and leave the trees on the periphery standing. There's your fifteen percent hold-back. It's still going to be a
clearcut."

"Except for the ones with orange," I said.

"Like I said. Supposedly." She made a face to show how far-
fetched this notion was. "They come in with their big rippin'
chainsaws and they get a hard-on for the cutting. It kills them to
leave anything standing. You'll see a lot of logs being hauled out
of here that have that orange mark."

Somehow, I don't know why, I was shocked at that. Not that
the companies would *want* to clearcut, or even that they'd be devi-
ous about the perimeter of the sale in order to get around saving a
mandated percentage. But that, once the boundaries had been
established—cut here, don't cut here—they'd do whatever they
pleased. *That* shocked me. I wanted to ask, *How can they get away
with that?* And then I thought about where we were, miles away
from the cheerful little picnic areas, and about who *wouldn't* be
there to see a thing, if Mudman and Starling and the others—and
now Neil and I—weren't here.

"But even if they leave them," she continued. "Let's just say they
do. The standing trees will probably die."

"Why?" I asked, shocked again.

"The temperature will rise ten to twenty degrees without the
other trees," Neil answered for her.

Starling nodded. She began to look more interested in Neil
and in what he obviously knew, but it didn't prompt her to ask
how he knew it. "They'll dry out, be more vulnerable to disease,
or fire, or wind damage," she added.

We were crossing a slippery series of branches someone had laid down to cross a trickling rivulet, and it was Starling, not Neil, who reached a hand out to steady me. I was grateful to her, but then embarrassed. I resolved not to look so tentative; if she could balance across them, so could I.

"I don't understand something," I told her. "You've got two platforms. What good does that do when they come, even if they leave you be up there? Won't they just cut all around you?" Too late I realized that the pronoun I chose didn't include me, as if I were merely an interested party come to take a tour, not an active participant.

If she noticed, she didn't show it.

"Sure." She shrugged. "But we've got some trees rigged with cargo nets so they can be occupied quickly. And there're always branches to sit on. Our strategies change fast according to the situation. Plus there's the publicity factor. It makes dramatic video when trees are falling all around a tree-sitter. The evening news likes it; it tends to get the middle-class environmentalists a little more engaged. They start making indignant calls to congressmen, stuff like that."

She halted abruptly in front of a pile of branches. I recognized it as one of the mysterious signals meant for those who knew.

"That's the entrance to one of our storage and equipment tunnels," she told us. "If our base camp gets cleared out by law enforcement—and it could anytime, you know—then we don't lose our stuff. In a way, the tools are more important than the manpower. We can always bring in more people, but it's almost impossible to resupply a site once it's being monitored."

My anonymity was sealed, then, upon learning that some rolls of barbed wire and bolt cutters and ropes and whatever else was stashed in the tunnels counted for more than each of us, than me. From my earliest memories I'd been told I was extraordinary, that my every drawing and wobbly letter was priceless. One of my mother's favorite complaints was about how unforgivingly she had been measured by her parents—the good grades unremarked upon, the occasional deviation from the superior range scrutinized, clucked over, like that C in penmanship in third grade. Their displeasure! Evening lessons with her mother ensued, copying the looping *f*'s, the thickets of lowercase *t*'s, each letter joining the next in an even chain of perfection. My mother has a beautiful hand. To copy it for my forged excuse notes meant I had to study the lessons of my dead Grandmother Prince, conform until my letters were as bland and uniform as the primer.

Ginnie would tell me how determined she was to have me learn differently, how my "self-esteem" would not suffer. My food would be praise, and my mother never stinted on my diet of it. She had succeeded in her programming efforts, I suppose, because the more I realized that I was required to keep my identity sealed inside, the more I suddenly itched to tell. Neil alone knew me here, most of the Julie there was to know, including the parts I pretended indifference to—the fact that I was two semesters from a Wellesley degree, that I would be summa cum laude if I stayed the course, that I was descended from Princes, Murdocks, and Whites who were judges and congressmen. I was special, according to the evidence of my whole life. None of it relevant here.

She was briefing us on the rules of engagement: If detained, if questioned, know nothing. You always act alone in the movement, she said. If taken into custody with another, know nothing about that other. Know nothing about what came before the moment in which you were apprehended. We were told to memorize the number of a certain lawyer who did pro bono work for the movement, and I wondered, if it came to it, whom would I call: my mother, or the stranger in Eugene. Neither, I decided. It would be Preston. I would give him the number of the movement lawyer and let him decide what to do.

But nothing I did that morning felt like crime. Filling sacks with fresh bread and fruit and vegetables and waving to the sitters at the top to pull them up was child's play. The ropes and platforms were Swiss Family Robinson stuff, the treehouse in the backyard I'd never had because we were city people. Starling said we could train to climb on the practice tree at base camp. Did we want to start in the trees or be part of the "elves" sabotaging the logging road?

I looked at Neil, assuming that whatever we'd do, we'd do together. "Let's climb," I said. Wasn't that, after all, what got me here? *How would you like to be fucked in the trees?*

He nodded, and Starling said, okay, she'd check with Mudman, but that we could train today and probably tree-sit tomorrow. Spiderman would teach us.

Back at base camp, Spiderman was gone; I took it he was off somewhere "monkey-wrenching," as they called it. We were told to wait for him before trying the practice tree, and in the meantime there wasn't a whole lot to do. We didn't know the woods well enough to scout yet, and the elves had the bulk of the action right now. I spent a couple of hours midmorning napping and drawing, the only type of documentation Mudman told me I was allowed. "No journals," he warned when he saw me take out my blank book. "You don't want a record of anything incriminating."

I held it up to show him a pencil sketch I'd begun in Yellowstone. A shaggy bison grazing head down, haunches at an angle that was, I suddenly realized, all wrong. That was the trouble with drawing for me. I had for years tried to break free of faithful representation into something looser, a line more consciousness-driven. But sketch after sketch turned into competent reproductions that failed in some hard-to-define way, the failure all the more apparent because it was clear that I had meant to draw the thing exactly as it was. My pencil would only move slowly, cautiously, searching for "correctness."

I began to draw Neil as he sat against a log talking to Mudman. I'd sketched him before and always ended up throwing what I did away. The little sideways expressions that fascinated me about him turned out, in my drawings, looking smug. I couldn't get the subtlety that I felt from his face, the play of intelligence and skepticism, the amusement that was always ready but was never unkind. Except watching him now, bent in conversation, I had a flow I liked. I wasn't even worrying about the face; I sketched the energy contained in his back as he leaned forward, elbows resting on his knees, head turned three-quarters away.

Neil loved to go on these talking jags about deforestation, all statistics and legislation and EPA policy and court decisions. I tuned him out a little when he was on that track, but Mudman was eating it up. Watching them so wrapped up in each other reminded me of that first night I found him at the frat party. Except then, once he'd gotten me in his radar I'd gradually pulled him out of that closed conversational circuit. Now he simply took for granted I was there in the background, waiting for him.

I must have dozed. I felt chilled, felt a presence too near me, and woke to the sight of a pair of dirty blue jeans standing inches from my face.

"She's not doing you any favors over here, man," the voice above me said.

Neil twisted around on his log.

"She's like a court reporter. Here's a picture of you, and your name written at the bottom, which I'm not going to say out loud, and the fucking date. Nothing like putting you at the scene or anything."

I turned my sketchbook face down as I tried to collect myself and scramble to my feet to face Spiderman. His mouth underneath the thick mustache was twisted in unfriendly amusement.

"Excuse me?" I said, my voice shaking a little. "Do you have some kind of problem with me?" I had a terrible urge to break into tears.

"Hey—" He shrugged. "You've got to learn some rules. It might be me you're putting next into your little court reporter book."

"Don't flatter yourself," I snapped. "And don't call it that. And don't stand over me like that again, either."

"Wait a second, relax, everybody." Mudman strode over to my side. "She didn't mean any harm, did you, Emerald?"

It took me a second to realize he was addressing me. *It's Julie,* I wanted to say, *and it's my business, and I don't need anyone to defend me.* Then I realized maybe I did.

Neil was there then, smiling at me, smiling all around. "Can I see?" he asked, lifting the sketchbook from my hand and squinting at it, pretending to assess its artistic merit. "It's good. It's for me, right, Em?"

How could he call me that so smoothly? How could losing himself and me be so totally fine with him?

"Actually it wasn't for you—" I bit the *Neil* from my tongue. "It was for me."

Neil made a little pout, then handed the book back. "Okay."

"Just erase the name and date, okay, Emerald? You don't know the kind of shitheads we're dealing with. Remember how badly they want to get us. For your protection and for all of ours, no names or dates." I remembered his earlier advice—"nothing incriminating"—and felt stupid, shamed, and condescended to all at the same time. I *did* have to learn how to fit in here, and maybe I wasn't trying very hard to. After the morning idyll of waking up to streaming sun and then carrying little picnics through the woods, the day had ground down to nothing but edgy waiting. The sun had disappeared behind a solid cover of clouds and the whole scene—the damp gloom, the ridiculous names—everything was getting on my nerves. I had on a flannel shirt beneath my sweatshirt, and it was June, but I still wasn't warm enough. Except for the fire last night, I hadn't been warm enough since I'd arrived.

"I'll remember," I said, trying to reclaim some dignity by looking Mudman squarely in the eye and ignoring Spiderman. I couldn't figure out where to put Neil in this scene. In some way, I'd felt obscurely made fun of by him.

"What's going on at the road?" Mudman asked Spiderman.

"We got in and out without being seen. But there'll be a reaction. We barricaded, and jammed up two pieces of equipment. General mischief was made."

"That's great." Mudman rubbed his hands together in anticipation and again I was reminded of a precocious child, with his smudged wire-framed glasses and cropped blond hair sticking up in several directions. His wrists were long and knobbed and barely downed with hair.

"What will they do?" Neil asked.

"The cops will come out looking. But they're not up to long treks in the woods unless they know where they're headed. Their style is to wait us out, try to get us in the open. The elves will split up and find their way back to base by circling around. We're fine here for now, but we can't have a fire tonight—too conspicuous."

After lunch Neil asked Spiderman to start our climb training, a lesson on using a rope looped over a branch to "self-belay" ourselves straight up off the ground. I wanted nothing more to do with him, but no one was asking me my preferences, so I sat down on a log—still huffy—and watched Spiderman rig Neil to a kind of harness seat. He showed Neil all the points of connection to buckle, and how to loop the rope around his foot.

"Okay, now pull on the rope so you're sitting in the harness, suspended."

Neil did as he was told and was soon bobbing in a seated position on an invisible cushion of air.

"This line's got give to it so you don't jerk to a stop if you fall," Spiderman said. "But it makes it a little harder to get going." His voice, now that he was teaching, was friendly and encouraging. His dark curly hair was a mass of tangles, matted in the back. Taller than Neil, he stooped over him slightly as he talked, his long fingers making shapes in the air as he gestured.

"Now let your looped foot come up a bit like it's in traction, then use your arms to pull on the rope and hoist yourself up while you push down with your leg."

Neil performed this move, at first slowly and clumsily, then with greater efficiency. I tried to pay attention so Spiderman could minimize his instruction to me when it was my turn.

"That's it, use the up-down motion of your leg to winch yourself up."

The two of us now had to lift our faces to watch Neil's ascent. He'd hang and bob for a minute, then his leg would rise, followed by his pulling arms, then the leg would push down, providing leverage for his trunk to rise; then he'd hang and bob some more. This tree was a fraction of the height of the ones we'd be climbing tomorrow, and he'd soon gotten up to the bottom branches.

"Coming down is easy," Spiderman shouted up. "Your leg is the brake. Let it out a little at a time."

Neil swung down in little jerks and too soon it was my turn. Neil grinned as he handed the harness over.

"Piece of cake," he said.

My fingers were trembling as I tried to do the buckling, and Spiderman watched and instructed, but didn't try to help. He handed me the loop and I put it around my own foot.

"Now pull tight on the line and sit down," he said.

I did and, magically, bobbed in midair as Neil had done.

Involuntarily I grinned, and Spiderman smiled back. Maybe he wasn't so bad.

I was worried I wouldn't have the upper body strength to pull myself up, but with the leverage of the leg pushing down at the same time, it wasn't as hard as I thought. It was work, but I could do it. When I'd managed to reach the bottom branches, I touched them for luck, and then began to lower myself down in little bobs. That part was fun. Neil gave me a little victory hoot as my toes touched ground, and I laughed a little as I fumbled to undo the harness, immensely relieved and slightly exhilarated at the same time. I glanced at Spiderman to see if he was sharing in any of this tiny triumph, since after all, he had taught us, but his face had turned carefully neutral behind his thick mustache, as if to warn me not to give myself too much credit for doing something as childishly simple as climbing a tree.

Later, as I helped a flat-faced girl with braids named Squirrel stir lentils and rice over the cookstove, I wanted the fire Mudman had forbidden us. The fire last night, the joint that had gone around, had made me feel that I was okay here, encircled by warmth and belonging with this strange collection of soldiers.

Don't be such a baby, I thought. *Like it's summer camp or something. Like someone's supposed to be showing you a good time.*

But still, I wanted that fire. I was cold and getting colder. Last night, flushed from the heat, sitting as close to the flames as I could, I'd felt my feelings of defensiveness melt away a little. Tonight, though, a kind of incredulity gripped me. The part about the cops was making me anxious and I knew, at bottom, I wasn't as committed as everyone else seemed to be. Back in Massachusetts, I'd caught Neil's fervor based on the arguments for preservation that seemed irrefutable and overwhelming. Then since I'd been in the woods I'd been moved by the actual beauty that was here to preserve, but now I was coming up against what this kind of idealism meant in practical costs. During moments of doubt, the voice of Ginnie rose loud in my head, judging the intelligence of these people, dismissing them as impressionable fanatics. Squirrel, with her dull concentration as she picked stones from lentils, looked to me like someone who'd made it to about the tenth grade. Uncharitably, I imagined that if she weren't here she'd be working behind the counter at a Burger King.

The lentils and rice were hot and I took seconds to fill the space I felt growing within me. Neil was at my side, but we had nothing much to say. Instead we listened to the subdued chat of the others—tonight everyone seemed a little dampened and less connected by the lack of a fire. I sat wearing my sleeping bag like a shawl, finally warm. I was too tired to care how my silence was construed. Mudman was telling us to expect Forest Service and trooper reconnaissance deeper into the cutting zone. They might discover our tree-sit positions in the old-growth stand by tomorrow.

"Emerald and River have volunteered to sit." Everyone looked at us, and under the pressure of their examination I tried to look enthusiastic.

"You guys know that if law enforcement's on the ground we can't resupply you or change shifts, right?"

Neil nodded seriously. I made a small assenting motion with my chin.

"We'll get you up there before dawn with plenty of food and water. Then we wait and see what they're up to. Mole, you're going up, too?"

A small, whiskery man, prematurely wizened by the elements, nodded smilingly. He looked older than the rest of us, maybe a weathered thirty-five. He wore a lumberjack coat and heavy worker-type boots, rather than the lightweight hikers the rest of us had.

"Let me go over what happens if you get arrested." Mudman looked levelly at Neil and me, but especially me.

"I did all that this morning," Starling interrupted. "You guys know the number and everything, right?" She turned back to Mudman. "They're fine."

I didn't like where this was going. Everyone seemed to be expecting us to be brought down from the trees and arrested tomorrow. As if everything had been merely in wait for the arrival of two new lambs for the slaughter. I said this later to Neil when we were huddled in our zipped-together sleeping bags under a blue tarp we'd strung up. There was no thought of making love. It was cold and damp, we were fully clothed, and the fresh air and anxiety had exhausted me.

"They just want us to be prepared," he whispered back. "It's going to be fine."

"No," I hissed. "They seem to be taking it as some kind of given. They have no loyalty to us. We arrive; they instigate an action and stick us in the trees to wait for retribution. Doesn't that feel like a conspiracy to you?"

"No. Of course they instigated an action. We were trying to get here in time to be in the thick of things, right? Well, we made it. We're involved. What did you expect?"

What did I expect? I realized that I expected to be seen for what I was. Someone supportive. Someone ready to fold leaflets or hold a sign or fill food buckets and wave, watching the picnic rise up to the fir canopy backlit by sky. I expected to be appreciated. Applauded, even. Certainly not sacrificed in some anonymous, worthless way.

It was too dark and I was too inexperienced to simply make my way through the woods and leave. Besides, what was out there for me but that deserted gravel road that went on for miles before reaching an area where there only *might* be other people around?

Somewhere near—within two or three miles—were cops and Forest Service—to the movement known as "Forest Disservice"— rangers. It could be done: Find the gravel road, then hope to run into the logging road where there would surely be a security force assembled. Announce myself as lost, in need of a safe ride to Eugene.

As if he felt the desperate roil of my thoughts, Neil began stroking my hair, whispering, "Shhh. It's going to be okay. I'm not going to let anything bad happen to you." He nuzzled closer, the curve of him cupping me, the warmth of his breath on my neck and ear. Our bodies were sealed together despite the thickness of clothes between us. "Go to sleep," he whispered. "You're brave and beautiful, and tomorrow night I'm going to make love to you in the trees."

My eyes were closed but I felt them prick with tears. I pressed my back into him and felt his hardness through our cloth layers. It was unbearable, all of a sudden, not to have him inside me. He was why I was here, and if I left I'd be leaving him. There was no middle way.

I was a selfish, spoiled rich girl who couldn't think of anyone besides herself, or anything besides her comfort and safety. Neil and the others weren't here on a lark. They were here because they believed in something.

It *was* beautiful here, and I *did* care that it not be ruined, or razed, or swallowed up. But did caring mean I had to offer myself up?

An owl hooted. My face was cold in a good way because the rest of me was so warmed.

He petted. My thoughts began to unkink one at a time until all I felt was Neil's broad, warm hand smoothing me, protecting me.

Owls hooted throughout the night, or I dreamed them. Slowly I came to understand their message. Each hoot was a call. What they cried without ceasing until dawn was, *"You, you. You, you."*

7

Someone was pushing me.

"No, shhh, it's just me, Starling. You guys have got to get up now."

It was still night and Starling was standing above me, holding out a plastic thermos cup. "Here. Have some tea."

Beside me Neil stretched and yawned and then silently scooted out of our bag. Reluctantly, I did, too. Shadowy figures were moving in the dark.

The tea was steaming and the insubstantial cup burned my fingers as I wrapped them around it. At home I drank from a set of mugs I had made my mother. They were rounded and heavy, curving out at the lip, and the clay I'd used had fired to a sandy yellow with bluish streaks. Drinking from one of them was like cradling a miniature earth, and you couldn't help holding it with two hands because it created such a feeling of balance and warmth and pleasure.

We had some instant oatmeal and then rolled our sleeping bags and tied them to our packs.

Starling grabbed me by the elbow. "I don't know if you want to, uh, use the 'facilities' or anything first." She gestured in the direction of woods. "It's not that there's not a provision for going up in the trees, but this is the last time you'll have your feet on solid ground for a while."

I shook my head, embarrassed. I wondered what the provision was. Hang your ass over the side? God.

The walk was warming, and between that and the tea and oatmeal I was feeling lithe and awake by the time we reached the old-growth stand.

Spiderman gave a low whistle, and I looked at him in appreciation. I didn't know what bird it was supposed to sound like, but with a long sliding note and two grace notes, the call sounded real.

There was an answering version from the trees, and I nudged Neil. Would he know how to do that sort of thing? He gave me a little smile. I could tell he was excited, and to tell the truth, I was, too.

The sitters had tied their packs to ropes and began lowering them down. Next a pair of jeaned legs appeared dangling over the side of the platform, then the body attached to them. In a series of little swinging bounces he was down, a long-haired guy with a bearded, sensitive face. He looked like a sheepish Jesus.

"Hey. Good to see you, man."

"All right. Nice job, Coot." Mudman clapped him on the back and began helping him unhook from the rigging.

"Coot, Emerald and River," Starling said, the unofficial hostess of the group. We nodded at each other.

A couple of others were soon down, Doe and Surfer.

"You two watch Mole go up. Then it'll be your turn."

Mole was halfway up his tree before I tuned in to the fact that I was supposed to be reviewing his technique. I was feeling increasingly unfocused and panicky, my breathing getting shallower, my limbs losing their warmth from the walk.

Then, too soon, Mole was up and pulling his pack up over the side of the platform. He had become one of the small waving half figures, gone from us.

"All set, River?" Neil's ascent was slower and more deliberate than Mole's, but still, he climbed steadily.

Then Neil's harness came down empty and our packs went up, and it was my turn.

The harness swinging in front of me before Mudman caught and held it reminded me of a noose.

"Can I do this?" I laughed nervously. The platform was ten times higher than the branches of the practice tree.

"Of course you can," Starling said soothingly. "It's just a little freaky the first time. After that, you'll be a pro."

I stood still, allowing her to buckle me in.

"What now?" My mind was suddenly blank.

"Just begin in a sitting position. There's no way you can hurt yourself," Mudman said.

I took a step back, breathing too quickly and getting no air. "I don't think—"

"Yeah, you can." Spiderman was at my elbow. "You did it yes-

terday, you can do it now. You just need to do it for longer is all."
He looped the line around my foot.

I pulled on the rope and sat, swinging a little in midair.

"Leg up. Now leg down and pull." I used my leg and arms and
hoisted myself up a short distance.

"There you go. That's all it is. Take as long as you want, no one
down here is in a hurry." Spiderman's voice was calm and encouraging and I had time to think what a puzzle he was while I
rested for a few seconds in between hoists. After I had been working awhile he shouted up, "You're halfway there." I heard him but
didn't look down, my thoughts swirling like a small cyclone of
leaves on the sidewalk. Bits of a poem from my lit class kept coming back to me senselessly: *Two small people, without dislike or suspicion.*
Leg up. Pull. Rest. Then a shard from the poem slicing in; *Why
should I climb the lookout?*

About two-thirds of the way up I was almost overwhelmed by
thoughts of the implacable insistence of gravity, how terrible the
pull of the earth is if you stop to receive it. I turned my head the
slightest bit toward the ground and, out of my peripheral vision,
saw the upturned heads, watching.

The monkeys make sorrowful noise overhead. I was almost to the
branches now, their reassuringly horizontal reach. Some were
thick enough to sit on, close enough to grab. I could see the white
plastic buckets tied to the edges of the platform like floats from a
raft. Starling had told us they were labeled with the provisions
they held, had briefed us on getting water from the rain catch,
had showed us how to light the small aluminum rocket stove.

"Doing fine," Neil said, looking over from above. "One more

will do it. Okay, there." Finally I was even with the platform and he told me to use the rope ladder to scramble over the side.

"I'm right here," he said, grabbing on to my harness to boost me over the edge. "You're home safe."

In a few seconds I was sprawled on the plywood, feeling the remaining adrenaline buzz through my limbs, and the leftover pressure of Neil's grip around my wrist. How had I ever just managed to do that?

"You were great," Neil said. He waved over the side and called down that we were all set.

Now that I was up, I doubted that I would ever manage to get down. I'd be here until some law-enforcement type came up and attempted to carry me down, and I knew with a bone-deep certainty that such an act wouldn't be possible. Gravity would gain the upper hand, we'd both fall to our deaths, the sheriff and I, and since I'd been breaking the law in the first place there'd be not a soul for my mother to sue.

8

Why should I climb the lookout? Now I remembered the rest of the poem that had haunted me on the way up the tree. The River Merchant's Wife, married off at fourteen, waits for her young husband to come back from an unknown place. I pictured her climbing the tower every day to search the distance, at first grievingly, then dutifully, filling in her days with watching until it was an industry, like Penelope's, shaped by emptiness. If her husband didn't return, then what? A girl in my Modern Poetry class was Chinese. She had a flamingo-pink streak in her hair and a pierced nose and spoke angrily about the status of women in China, how the River Merchant's Wife would be nothing without him, how she was sure that if the husband didn't come back the girl's life would be over. *Why should I climb the lookout?* Maybe for the view of distance itself, which, like the one I had from the platform, could perhaps make the world come into focus in a whole new way.

I could see for a mile or two, though it was a view through branches, a Cubist collage. Looking east, where the sun was rising peach over the hilltops, I saw the clearcut zone in the distance like the shaved hide of a lamb, like a raw skin of the earth. The cutting was brutally complete, stubbled only with stumps and discarded branches.

"Oh, my God," I said to Neil, pointing.

He looked at me as if he weren't sure what planet I'd come from. "You've never seen it?" he asked. "What about all those websites I showed you? What about the drive up?"

"I didn't see it on the drive up," I protested. Now that he mentioned it, I did remember some talk about the Eagle Run cut, Shaman gesturing off the road to the hills in the distance. Did I see it? I'd been too frightened of Shaman himself, staring at the buckskin lace around his gray hair, trying to get the meaning of it, and of why I was being taken somewhere by him. And the websites? Pixels. Neil had always been showing me photos on the computer, and I'd always been seeing them. But I hadn't.

The barrenness of the clearcut in front of me was so total, so authoritative, that I knew immediately our chances of saving this tree or any other were nil. Some cruelly efficient force had done that, and would continue doing it. Now that I saw it for myself, really *saw* it, I wondered how they could let anyone do something so obviously devastating. *Who's in charge?* Couldn't they just bring the governor out here or something and show him? It brought home to me how little I had actually listened to the rhetoric of the movement up to now, how naively assuming I still was that all the authority structures were in place to protect me and every-thing else that mattered.

If you swiveled your view off to the side, the hills were unscarred and fully green, tufted with distance like a chenille spread, though Neil pointed out that most of it was second growth—tree farms, really—no biodiversity, no hardwoods to hold in the moisture to naturally reduce fire damage, or trees tall enough for the vanishing species that depended on the old-growth canopy. I'd heard over and over again that only one percent of old growth remained, but the words, the numerical importance of them, had always slipped by me like a breeze. Now I was gripped by the thought of how lit-tle one percent was, how irrevocable its loss would be. The air this high was incredibly sweet, less mossy and damp than on the ground. I made a resolve to start learning the names of the birds around me, because through the blend of song, I began to follow the threads of different calls. I could understand how Spiderman might have sat up here for days and practiced that long sliding note and two chirping short ones until he had them exactly right.

I wondered if the cell phone would work from here, if my mother would think I was crazy for holding it out to the air and letting her hear the birds. But then she'd let me know how upset she was about what I was doing and try to talk me down, and I couldn't risk her ruining this.

I settled for listening in silence with Neil, knowing we'd never be able to convey the essence of this moment to others. They'd tune us out the way I sometimes tuned Neil out. This must be what the bond was about in the movement. The not being able to fully articulate what was here, what was worth saving. To tell it was to either fall into clichés or come off sounding nutty.

We could see Mole twenty yards over in his tree, and he'd waved, then sat down to read with his back to us. I had the feeling he was respecting our privacy, that he knew what the first morning was like. The support crew on the ground had long since made their way back to base, and I felt perfectly alone with Neil, with our tree.

Everyone else referred to it as "Maia." That's going way too far, I'd thought. Aliases for people, okay. But a tree is a tree, and I'm not giving it a name.

We swayed ever so slightly, the ropes lashed to our platform creaking, and it felt oddly like being at sea, a sea full of life and depth. The tree we were perched on was maybe five hundred to seven hundred years old. Neil had already spotted nests in some of the branches, and while some of them might be abandoned, I could hear a rustle and swoop of activity around one. I didn't, that morning, call the tree Maia, but after a couple of nights of being rocked to sleep in its branches I did.

"There. You see them?" Neil put his hand on my forearm and pointed. Through the branches I could just make out something yellow crawling into view.

"That's the new logging road," he said.

"How long before they get to the cutting zone?"

He shrugged. "Two days? Three?"

"It looks like they fixed their equipment."

"Or brought in new, who knows."

We watched the ingress of the toy feller as it scraped a path one tree at a time. It would back away and then some piece with a grappling hook would drag the tree out like a body. From our vantage point we could see the operation only in glimpses. I thought of a little boy I'd occasionally babysat on the Vineyard, how he would bulldoze his trucks through his mother's garden, liking nothing better than to flatten things in slow motion, making humming, intent noises as he watched his progress. Even as I'd encouraged him to make a detour around the irises, I'd loved how his play was work, that it was serious. He was only two and I had seen that seriousness as evidence of his intelligence.

We couldn't hear the rumble of equipment in the distance yet, but I knew the birds wouldn't be there anymore. They would have lifted off in a single wave of startled silence.

What of the nests?

Perhaps the birds with eggs or nestlings stayed on, fluttering and calling out and beating useless circles around the noise and machines, making darting, desperate flights from perch to perch as the felled trees were dragged away.

I turned away from the yellow toys crawling a fraction of an inch at a time in our direction, trying to shut them out, and set about unrolling our sleeping bags and making a little camp. If I didn't look down over the railing of rope and branches, and I tried not to, it almost seemed we were in a little room. The platform, about six by nine feet, was already furnished with a "library" of paperbacks lined up on a shelf made of tied-together bark. A plastic milk crate held the stove and a few pots and dishes. Bundled overhead and lashed to a branch was a roof tarp you could unroll and tie to an opposing branch for shade or protection from the rain. In addition to the sandwiches and fruit Starling had sent up in our packs, there was an array of grains, beans, pastas, condiments, and oils in the plastic buckets secured to the sides of the platform. It was as if everyone who had been here before us had added his or her own particular piece of housekeeping.

We stretched out on the sleeping bags, looking up at the fili-gree of branches. Today was warmer—maybe just because we were up high—the sun hazed over by a thin layer of clouds that was already burning off. I'd arranged my heavy sweater under my head for a pillow and, in a fit of resolve to quit looking after Neil, had provided nothing for him, waiting to see if he would do it for himself. He didn't, and in a move that annoyed me for some rea-son, merely folded his arms beneath his head to cushion it, his elbow jutting into the space that was too close to my right ear until I shifted a few inches to the left. Maybe what annoyed me most was that he didn't even seem conscious of the fact that I'd neglected to put a pillow out for him, just as he'd have been unconscious of the favor if I'd had. Yet he was perfectly at his ease, not needing, after all, any ministration from me. That was a lesson in itself. It seemed like I was continually providing some half of a bargain he had no interest in. Or that I was acting out some script I never consciously chose. Nurture, provide.

What was so bad about that? There were the birds—I imag-ined female birds, but what I knew about bird family life was zip—bound to their nests, their young. They had scripts to fol-low, clear and insistent ones.

Neil seemed only loosely bound to the personal, to the idea of other people. It shocked me a little—*me*, with my fraught relation-ship to my mother—that he had so little contact with his family. His sister Holly was a sociology major at Oberlin, and his parents still lived in Lowell, where he'd been raised. Though he lived within an hour's drive of them, he only saw them a handful of times a year, at holidays. When I'd asked him why, he'd shrugged, claimed busyness with his thesis. I'd pressed him for evidence of childhood traumas at the hands of his parents, fallings out, long-standing rifts, but he denied having any. The fact was he just didn't seem to need a lot of contact with his family. There were times I suspected he didn't need me, either. Not that he didn't *want* me in some fairly intense way. But was I required? Most of the time I felt him hungering instead for an engagement with his beliefs—a way to ground his actions in them. Well, he was finally here. I was on the point of asking him if it felt like the way he'd hoped it would, but when I glanced at him, his gaze directed up into the branches, the moment seemed wrong for talk.

Time began to slow then. At first I felt like I had to be doing something, like I should sketch or—fuck you, Spiderman and Mudman—write a letter or journal entry, or maybe a poem. Like the time had to be used for it to be real. Neil's peace next to me, his willingness to be still, made me too self-conscious to go digging for paper, so I lay still, too, until keeping busy began to seem a quaint notion, one wholly beside the point. Drowsy from breezes and feathery rays of sun, I drifted but didn't quite sleep. I felt perfectly safe, as long as I lay stretched out between Neil and the tree trunk, and I was lulled by a swaying sensation, perhaps imagined. It was almost like being in a kind of lucid dreaming stage that felt perfectly aware of where I was, but let me float and be other places at the same time.

I couldn't quite let go of the frame of my mother's vision—*what would she think if she saw us now?*—as if I could foster no clarity of my own unless I borrowed her point of view. That I felt that her point of view was so neatly folded into my own was galling, but I'd always been able to conjure her inside me like this, whether I wanted her there or not.

Would I ever tell her about this, really make her understand? For some reason, I longed to, felt the tale building inside like when my younger self would burst into the house with news. *Guess what, Mommy, Frannie Price got a dog! And she said I could help walk it! Mom, James Seeley nominated me to be room rep! And I won!*

She'd replied to my exclamations with ones of her own. We'd shared a full happiness in those moments. But it had been a long time since I'd brought anything like that to her, a delicate soap bubble of excitement. When I got the art award at the Briar School, I didn't come home brimming with the news. Instead I left the letter the headmistress had given me open on the kitchen table for her to find. I would never dream of showing her the notebook I'd filled with poems at Wellesley, or telling her that my workshop teacher had said a couple of my things might be publishable. I had systematically engineered a remoteness between us, like a vast plain she'd need a compass to find me across.

But what if I said: *I'm calling you from a tree, Mother. Neil's here. We've both changed our names. I see the logging machines making their way toward us in the distance. I can't hear them yet. I can only hear birds, everywhere. It's incredible.*

The facts would never tell her about the exhilaration, the peace, the *rightness* of this action. My panic of the night and during the climb had evaporated. I knew I was lucky to have been brought, in spite of myself—in spite of my background and my selfishness and my fears—to this moment. My mother would see it as delusion. She wouldn't exclaim, at least not the way I'd want her to. She'd find it necessary to tell me, in biting detail, how she thought I was being used, what I was in for.

9

We finally roused ourselves, hungry. I had a watch in my backpack, but didn't feel like checking it. So what if it was only nine o'clock, or ten? We were starved.

"PB and J or PB and J?" I offered.

Neil reached over for his sandwich. Over on his own platform, Mole looked to be sleeping.

"What do you think his story is?" I asked Neil, tearing off a bite of my sandwich like some ravenous dog. I hoped they'd packed a dozen for us. Each.

"He's been around. At least ten years in the movement—joining in actions from Washington state to California. Did you know he used to be a logger?"

I raised my eyebrows but my mouth was too full to reply. When I'd taken a swig of water to unstick it, I said, "He told you that?"

Neil shook his head. "Mudman. He was saying how much he trusted Mole, that he'd been arrested I don't know how many times, a dozen or something."

I rolled my eyes. "I wish you guys would quit referring to arrests like they were merit badges or something. Let's strive to *avoid* arrest, okay?"

"Why, so you can keep your résumé nice and clean? For what?"

I was stung by his tone. I hadn't talked about any particular ambitions with Neil, but that didn't mean I wouldn't have any someday. I didn't trust myself yet with the vague notions I had of getting an MFA—maybe in writing, maybe in art. I sort of wanted both, and figured that made me too much of a dilettante to deserve either. Wasn't a *real* artist or a *real* writer supposed to know what she needed to do? I had the notion that it was like love, and that if you had doubts, it wasn't authentic.

When I didn't answer him, Neil looked at me with the rueful sideways smile that he used as apology.

"No, you should. Do something big, I mean," he said.

He was confusing me. "You, too," I said.

"I am. This feels big to me. This feels much bigger than researching it from a distance." He shook his head, disgusted. "I mean, what is it that I thought I was serving back in Cambridge, completely detached from"—he gestured—"all this? The cause? No way. Academics—take my advisor, for a start—are too busy serving themselves to be of any use in the real world. Narcissistic bullshitters. This is what's real. You see?"

"I guess. But that doesn't mean I want to get arrested. The whole idea scares me to death. Don't tell me you *want* to."

"I'm not afraid to."

"That's what scares me the most. Like I'll be following your lead and you'll be somehow going out of your way to get us dragged in."

"I won't." He shook his head. "I wouldn't do that to you."

I looked at his eyes to see if he meant it. He put his sandwich down and reached for me. Then, amid crumbs and in full light he was pulling my sweatshirt up and I was undoing his jeans buttons. I tucked my bare legs into a sleeping bag, glancing off to the side to make sure Mole was still asleep. I stroked Neil, our unwashed smells rising up to us, sharp and personal against the sweet backdrop of the woods. We made slow love in the trees. When I came, I imagined that falling wouldn't be straight down at all, but a leisurely, dizzying spinning like we got from those maple seedpods we'd called "helicopters" as kids.

As we smoothed ourselves back together I was relieved to see Mole still prone, his head facing away from us. I collected our crumbs and arranged them in a row along one edge of the platform. In a few seconds, some birds came swooping closer, checking us out. Finally a bold one dashed in for a morsel and soared away with its prize. Then another. When they became accustomed to the notion that we'd remain motionless, they paused before flying off to cock their heads back and swallow, daring us to make a move. Then a couple of them remained in place, treating themselves to a buffet, and I wished I'd dug out my guidebook before spreading the bread crumbs. As they hopped along the wood, I tried to memorize the yellow eye ring, the full chest, the darker feathers on their backs and the mottled brown feathers on their throats so I could look them up. They ate and flapped up to a higher branch, calling, *whit, whit,* from their sanctuary.

We flopped down on our stomachs and read the paperbacks

we'd brought with us, Thoreau for Neil, and George Eliot for me. My eyes kept stalling on the page; I couldn't keep my mind on Dorothea. She was too sensible, too level and good. But for all that, she was stupid. Couldn't she see through Casaubon, the dry old stick? Did she really think so little of herself that warming his milk and refilling his inkpots was enough? Instead of finishing a page I pictured Neil's body—that smooth hollow at the base of his back where I put my hand when he was inside me. I loved the elegance of his leg muscles, how they suggested quickness, a readiness to spring. Sometimes on the weekends we had run together, and I could always feel his speed held in check for my sake. He never showed that he minded running at my pace, but when we finished my two miles and he dropped me back at his porch before finishing his five, he'd speed away as if suddenly released.

I became conscious of the whine of the machines, still distant. I nudged him. "Listen."

He lifted his head and we waited. Then we heard it again, a faraway needling, mosquitolike. The loggers had been out of sight for an hour or more, hidden by some dip in the landscape or density of trees.

"They're far away," Neil said, cocking an ear to listen and then lowering his gaze back to his book. Then, "Listen to this, is this not perfect?"

He read out a passage from his book, the editor describing how Thoreau had been jailed for not paying a poll tax to a government that supported slavery and waged war on Mexico. When Emerson had come to visit him in his cell, he'd said, "Henry, what are you doing in *there?*" To which Thoreau had reportedly replied, "Waldo, what are *you* doing out *there?*"

"It's just so true—it's really that stark, you know? You're either in the system or out of it, no having it both ways. That guy was brilliant."

I dimly remembered my freshman lit teacher telling us that Thoreau's shack in the woods was an easy walk from Concord and that he often strolled to town to dine at the homes of his middle-class friends. It seemed pointlessly argumentative to mention this, so I tried to go back to my reading, but Dorothea interested me even less now. So sure of herself, so sure of the right thing. What if the right thing was the wrong thing? What if you could no longer tell which was which?

I put down my book and lay my head on my sleeping bag, feeling a great tiredness I couldn't have explained. Neil put down his Thoreau and started kneading my shoulders. Then he stopped and turned me on my side away from him, curving his arms around me and shaping his body to fit mine. We lay like that a long time, neither of us speaking, while the birds erupted inter-mittently in a slurry of song and the tiny drone of the machine was sometimes audible, sometimes not.

I rolled back around to face him so that our knees jutted together and we held a roundness of space between us. I'd been thinking again of Sara, my best friend when I was still at Montessori school, before Briar. I realized it was a resemblance in Starling's round face that had been nagging me. Sara and I had been inseparable since we'd napped side by side in preschool; I'd spent so much time with her family that they were almost surro-gates to me. By fourth grade Sara's big thing was horses, and on Saturdays I'd go with her to the stable to help her groom her show horse. I was telling this to Neil, nostalgically, I guess.

"She had her own horse?"

"She and her sister each had one. Sara's was a bay with white stockings. She'd brush Little on one side, and I'd brush her on the other. What seems weird to me now was how comfortable we were taking care of this huge animal. I mean, we each weighed seventy-five pounds. And Little weighed, I don't know, nine hundred pounds or something. But we had no fear of her whatsoever."

Neil gave his head a little shake.

"What?" I asked, thinking he didn't believe me.

"Just your world. Show horses. Private schools. It's nothing like what I came from."

"It's not like we were rich," I said. "I didn't keep a horse."

"But you grew up around it. You didn't see anything out of the ordinary in it."

"No, but I didn't see anything out of the ordinary with my mom working, either."

"Did she have to work?"

I sat up and hugged my knees, then shrugged. To me this wasn't the important thing. "My grandfather left some trusts. The point was she wouldn't have been satisfied *not* to work." It was ironic how I was claiming this as a source of pride when my mother's work had so often bugged me as a child, coming, as it had always seemed to, before me.

"What about your father? You've never told me about him."

"Nothing to tell." For some reason it had been easy to tell Frida about my sperm-bank daddy. With her I could even joke about his possible identities. We'd gone bowling together once, which I was inexplicably good at, and she'd accused me of having a professional in my genes, his name—"Al" or "Rog"—stitched in cursive on his league shirts. We'd wondered if his sperm donations had been a regular thing in between tournaments, and if I had a couple of dozen half-siblings walking around, each as skilled with a bowling ball as I.

"You'd better take care not to marry one," she'd warned. "Take every boyfriend bowling and check him out."

All I'd told Neil was that my parents weren't together, the truth. Something about the all-American symmetry of his family—even the name of the street he'd grown up on, Arcadia—felt like an obscure challenge to my paltry family of two.

"When did they get divorced?"

Did I have an obligation to correct an assumption? I decided I didn't.

"I have no memory of him. She doesn't talk about it." Both statements also technically true. I'd intended to tell Neil sometime about how I came into the world, but kept hanging back out of a sense of loyalty to my mother. After all, it was her business. Mine, too, of course. Insofar as I could, I'd tried to make my peace with the facts, which is not to say it didn't feel a little tender to open up to Neil's probing. Frida's joking, on the other hand, was a kind of balm to me. It was as if she occupied my position, and the joke was on all of us together.

He rolled on his back and lay silent for a minute, during which time I felt the conversation ebbing away, both of us retreating to our own thoughts. Why shut him out? I suddenly wondered. On impulse, maybe to draw him back to me, I said, "Actually, my mother was never married."

He lifted his head to prop it on an elbow, brows raised.

I hugged my knees tighter and tried to frame some words of explanation, a silly, embarrassed smile playing on my face. Why should it embarrass me that I had no father? How was that anything I'd been able to help?

I shook my head in response to some unspoken query. "There's nothing to tell. That's the problem. I mean, not problem. It's just that Ginnie didn't have me with anyone. She got herself artificially inseminated."

He nodded once. No mockery in his expression, not even the amused squint that had first captured me at the M.I.T. party. He was simply taking it in. In the lemony light that filtered through the branches, his face had no edges.

It seemed stingy not to give him more, so I continued, "She didn't know the donor or anything. It was one of those places you go."

One afternoon in second grade when Preston had collected me from school and was walking me back to the office to wait for my mother, I'd taken the opportunity to confirm something I'd been privately convinced of ever since I'd been old enough to consider the subject. Preston was my father. He had to be—hadn't I known him ever since I could remember? (Glimpses of myself in a striped toddler's overall, going somewhere perched on his mountain-high shoulders. Preschool, a party dress, Preston applying some thrillingly serious gauze and tape to a bloody scrape on my knee, then daubing the blood spot from the hem with a soggy paper towel until there was only a pink ghost of a stain he assured me no one would notice.) During that walk home I'd slipped my hand in his confidingly, and moved in jerky little steps to avoid breaking my mother's back on the sidewalk cracks. I'd come right out and told him that I knew, and it seems now, in memory, that he took a long time to answer, so long that I'd already saved my mother innumerable times with my bunched-together, crablike steps, each time breaking the synchrony of our stride and causing erratic little tugs on his wrist.

"No, Julie," he'd finally said. "I'm not your father, though it would be a great honor to be. I'm something else, though, something permanent and very special. Besides being your friend, and your mother's friend, which I most certainly am, I'm your guardian. That means that, after your mother, I'm the one who would take care of you."

After the initial vertigo of loss—I'd been so certain, and if not Preston, then no one, no father—I grew to like the sound of it: Guardian. It sounded like something very solid, no room for anything to go wrong. Preston must have reported the conversation, because later my mother corroborated everything he'd said without my asking her: that if she was ever sick or—she could not bring herself to say, but I knew what she was leaving out, children instinctively ready to embrace the morbid—*dead*, Preston would take care of me.

I quit looking, then, for signs of my face in his, which were quite different from each other, after all. His broad forehead under a curling forelock of red hair, versus my long, thin face framed (half hidden) by brown, straight hair. Preston had what I thought of as a president's profile—defined in bold strokes, with large, decisive features—whereas my own seemed to me, the longer I stared at it in our bathroom mirror, a smudged thumbprint of a face, the features blurring together until I could no longer see anything that made me distinctive at all. There was a stranger in that face somewhere, muddying the resemblance to my mother that people always claimed was so immediately visible, but I would never be able to pick out his pieces and assemble them into a portrait.

"Wow." Neil looked at me with a little smile. "That's kind of heavy, huh? Why'd she go and do a thing like that?"

Though his expression was kind and interested, I bristled at the words. Why shouldn't she, if she wanted to? Asking it was like proposing the erasure of me—even though I'd asked my mother exactly that. Repeatedly, in fact.

"Jules," she'd just say, shaking her head, as if she were helpless before my need to get to the bottom of a question that wasn't fully covered by available speech. "I wanted you. So much. I had this idea of you, and the question was how to get you, make you real." Often these conversations had taken place in her queen bed, where I'd slip in during the early morning hours if the light in my own room felt too charcoal-grainy to be awake in, and too menacing for continued sleep. As the light brightened into something familiar, we'd wake slowly, luxuriously toasty in our tangle of flannel nightgowns, and at those times I couldn't imagine a third person, a father, sharing that warmth. Having a Preston, a Guardian, was just right, a sentry outside our private union.

At moments like these I'd sometimes ask again to hear the story of my birth, which had grown in detail as I'd gotten older, so that the version I had in my head now was the one with all the woman-to-woman flourishes—the natural labor and delivery, coached by Maura, that Ginnie, who had jogged until the seventh month, approached like an athletic feat. Though she bragged of her Lamaze breathing, her refusal of drugs (admitting to just one small episode of screaming during transition), she also—perhaps to warn me off of trying it myself too early—said she thought that near the end she was convinced she'd never make it, that she was simply going to break apart. I couldn't picture my mother screaming, or in any way undone, and didn't like to try. I'd hurry her forward from the pain part to tell about what I liked hearing best, those first few hours in the hospital when we'd drifted together on an air mattress of drowse and undrugged euphoria.

That was before I had a name. She told me she'd studied my face, all that showed of me in the capsule of swaddling, and tried to match it to something suitable from her short list. Ginnie believed in staying within the latitude and longitude of ancestral naming as a way of locating oneself in the world, however vexed certain of those family coordinates might be. I might have been a Rose, her mother's name; or an Elizabeth, after a great-aunt (and manifold with choices I liked: Liz, Liza, Eliza, Beth, Bette, and on and on); or a Charlotte, after my great-grandmother. In the end, the search for appropriate meaning won out. Rose (though she was tempted, she said, my face, my fists, like tight pink buds) ulti-mately sounded too delicate for a daughter of Ginnie Prince. Charlotte (Fr. "little and womanly") and Liza (Heb. "pledged to God") also had to go for their dependent undertones. And so I was named Julia (Lat. "youthful"), after an aunt my mother had never met who had died of influenza before she was born.

She confessed she'd never dreamed it was possible to love another being so much—and I fell in love with that newborn, too, the way she described me: softly mewing and draped across her chest, skin to skin; my noncolicky, wholly quiescent self being passed from one set of visiting arms to another, charming the company with darting minnow smiles and mercurially expressive eyebrows. It was new to her, this feeling oneself so entirely pledged to another life. That was when, she said, she first thought of the guardianship. It gave her peace as soon as Preston agreed, a reprieve from a sudden intimation of her own mortality, as if the parturitional door that had opened to admit me to the world had sealed imperfectly, the weatherstripping between this side of life and the other coming loose just enough to let in a small, cold draft reminding her of her ordinary, limited life span. I would survive her; I was supposed to: the inheritance ensured by the lifetime's supply of minuscule eggs already folded inside me—an infinite supply, really, when you considered the whorled futures it lay within my own power to spawn, daughters of my own, and theirs.

With Preston in place to buffer us against catastrophe, the arrangement felt complete to Ginnie, this symmetrical mirroring of a mother, a daughter.

But still I'd ask her about it again, maybe months later, as if the answer might have changed or added new proofs, something about the equation of *mother* + *no one* = *Julie* never feeling finished to me, or true.

"She wanted me," I told Neil. "That's why."

Neil rolled back abruptly, crossing arms behind his head, as if my answer too neatly settled it. I thought he was finished with the question of me and my unorthodox conception until he said, "That makes you lucky, then. You didn't miss a thing."

"I guess not, not really." He'd seemed to change the subject to himself by implication, but I didn't know what to ask or how to comment, he'd always been so cursory on the subject of family.

After a few moments, I asked, "Did you give your parents the whole story about being here? The illegal stuff?"

"I guess they know." He was still looking straight up, studying the crossed pattern of branches above.

"And they're cool with all that?"

"Probably not," he said.

"They don't argue with you about it?"

He shrugged his shoulders. "What good would it do?" Then he rose up again on one elbow and looked at me with the version of his amused smile that sometimes felt patronizing. "I'm a big boy, right? On my own in all respects, no trust fund or any other apron strings to keep me in line."

I made a small noise of impatience and he held out one hand to quiet me. "No, I think it's great. Why wouldn't you love it? I'm just saying—and remember, I'm seven years older than you—I'm alone."

I decided not to take issue with his choice of the word *alone*, its insinuation that we were nothing to one another, and said instead, "It's just so strange the way you talk about them."

"What way?"

"Like they're acquaintances. Like they're perfectly pleasant people you don't know very well."

"Of course I know them. How could I not know them?"

"Do you *like* them?"

"They're good people."

"Good people you're not close to. Which strikes me as odd. They don't seem to be, I don't know, *presences* you walk around with, the way my mother rattles around inside my head whether I want her there or not."

"I don't channel them, J," he teased. Neil used to call me J before he started calling me Em for the benefit of our movement comrades. Score one for the home team, I thought.

"I don't *try* to channel my mother," I said. "But sometimes it's like she's not even a separate person. It's hard to explain."

"Maybe because it's been just the two of you."

"Well, yeah, sure. But I've had plenty of friends from normal-sized families like yours and still there's an *intensity* there, whether it's love or hate, which is just missing when you talk about your family. It's scary."

"Everything's 'scary,' with you." He smiled, reaching for the slight mound of my breast beneath my sweatshirt. I batted his hand away.

"Don't mock."

"I'm not mocking."

"Yes, you are."

"All right, so I'm not particularly close to my parents. Lots of people aren't. Big deal. It doesn't mean anything except we don't quite see eye to eye."

I was silent for a few seconds, listening to a crow caw nearby, strident and challenging and somehow comic at the same time.

"My dad is a PE teacher and a coach," he resumed. "Do you have any idea what that means?"

"Well, yeah," I said. But I didn't. His voice had an edge that seemed entirely out of proportion to the statement.

"It means," he continued, as if I hadn't spoken, "that certain things are important to him. Vitally, bizarrely important. Like throwing and catching balls. Kicking balls. These things are important to him."

"You're athletic," I said, thinking of his body in motion as he ran, pulling ahead, away from me. "You run like a cheetah."

He shook his head impatiently. "With my father, it's games. Winning and losing games. This whole weird tribal thing: the ball throwers and the ball throwers' watchers. I could never see the point of it—imagine, the coach's son—and it drove him nuts."

"He gave you a hard time?"

"Not in the way you mean. But I knew he couldn't stand it. Always trying to get me to put down a book or get off the computer and play a game of catch. He'd nag me to come outside and 'toss a few around.' Then he'd pitch—nice and soft, I could tell he was holding way back—and the ball would go right past me. I'd walk to go get it—you know, kind of dragging my feet to send a message—and he'd say in that big encouraging coach voice, 'That's okay, Neil, hustle after it!' Then after about ten minutes, he'd give up and say in a disgusted tone, 'Go ahead, get out of here.'"

Another crow cawed, or maybe it was the same one, mimicking, it seemed, the sour note of Coach Davidson's abrupt dismissal: *Get out of here, go.*

"It sounds like he was just trying to connect with you, and that's the only way he knew how."

"Of course he was. I just couldn't . . . *do* it." Neil shrugged helplessly. Then he gave a short laugh. "Holly could. She got him off my back."

"She likes sports?"

"Yeah. Varsity basketball her freshman year. *Go, Holly!*"

"So . . . fine, right? Different drummer, and all that? It sounds like it worked itself out; Dad got his ballplayer, and you got left alone."

He gave a short bark of laughter. "Yeah, that's about right."

"What do you mean?"

He draped an arm across his forehead as though to block the sun, though the light was dappled and gentle.

"Oh, I don't know. How'd we get talking about this shit, anyway? *Alone.* It's just how I've always felt. It's my own fucked-up, crazy trip. Of course it's not my parents' fault. Like I said, they're solid, God-fearing Americans: concerned parents, active community members, moderate Republicans, loyal fans of the home teams. Blah, blah, blah. If I had allowed them to put me in Cub Scouts they would have been the den leaders, you know what I'm saying? Good eggs."

I stared at him, at what I could see of his shielded face, feeling perplexed. Handsome, he was surely that. Very bright—even brilliant—without a doubt. When I'd first seen him that night at the M.I.T. party he'd seemed so utterly sure of himself, the confident center of the most interesting conversation. Of course, that conversation, like most that he starred in, consisted of numbers, statistics, policies, legislation. Frida and I had always joked about M.I.T. boys and their scary-smart intensity—many had a near-autistic inability to make eye contact and inconsequential small talk. Their hold on the social world was often tenuous, but the best of them honed both their gifts and their deficits into a laser-like mastery of the universe, an eccentric charisma. I had immediately placed Neil in this group.

But now I flashed on a vision of Neil as a solitary boy on the sidelines watching the way the rest of the kids formed an easy band of banter and showmanship, the whole thing somehow flowing too fast for him. I remembered how the boys at my elementary school would go screaming out of the building at recess, skidding across the gravel to arrive first at the painted four-square lines or the net bag of playground balls. If you weren't part of it, it could be a terrifying spectacle. It was true; the rituals of the tribe, the channeling of its violent energies, depended heavily on the use of balls.

"I'm sure your dad was proud of you for your science stuff, your M.I.T. scholarship and all that. He must have finally begun to *get* you."

"Yeah, it got to a point where he saw that having a geek for a son might pay off." He snorted. "Everything's cool if you get some prize or certificate for it, right?"

"The geeks were actually the cutting edge of cool when I got to high school. The jocks were still deluded about themselves and their futures, but the guys tapping away in the computer room, writing code—they were the ones who were going to change the world. You were one of *them*, weren't you?"

"I guess, maybe," he conceded. "Not one of the entrepreneurial geeks, though. Those guys were all about money. I was a SIFOPE geek."

"SI—?

"Students in Favor of Preserving Earth," he intoned with the flicker of a smile.

"Nice name."

"Wasn't it? I can't take credit, though. Sasha Lieberman was the founder, president, and recruiter."

There was something melting in his tone when he said that name, something that alerted me. I pictured a skinny, intense girl with quirky clothes like someone I'd known at the Briar School who'd worn an old fishing hat studded with buttons warning of global warming, the extinction of owls, thinning ozone, and blackened coral reefs. On her, it looked chic. That would have been Sasha.

"Let me guess. You and Sasha were an item," I said, keeping my voice light.

He glanced at me, then rolled on his back and stretched elaborately. "For a time," he admitted.

"What happened?"

"She went to Yale."

Something about his disinclination to elaborate made me suspect all the more that she'd been it, the one who mattered, the one who'd left him. He was silent, studying the lattice of branches above him, maybe recalling how the alchemy of his first intellectual and physical passion had been lubed by the sweet, oysterish vaginal juices of Sasha Lieberman. I couldn't help it; I pictured them staying late to clean up after their meetings, their energetic fucking on some crumb-riddled couch of a Student Activities Office. I tried to banish these thoughts with the fact that it was me, now, sharing the tree platform with him. Us, together, in this fallen Eden.

I suddenly felt cramped and stiff in my sitting position. With deliberate slowness, I straightened and did a few gentle twists of my trunk before nonchalantly turning to face away from him, lying on my side and letting a small, manipulative silence fall.

Immediately he turned in my direction and flung an arm around me, taking the bait.

"You were close to her," I said in a small voice that, even to my ears, sounded horribly girlish and aggrieved.

"Define *close*," he said, snuggling in.

"Oh, brother. Never mind." I tried to put a space between us but he wouldn't let me.

"Right now," he said, almost whispering, "I feel very close to you." His lips were brushing my hair, then my ear, and I felt the warm, pulsing energy return where he'd just been a couple hours before, where I was already wet from him. As we kissed and pressed ourselves together, I couldn't help thinking about his question, what we meant, each of us in our hunger, by *close*. By *right now*. Whether *now* was a moment that slid forward with us in time, a constancy of the present, or whether it had ticked away already, like the day that was becoming, had already largely become, the past.

10

We stayed in the tree six days, but calendar time became irrelevant. My awareness of circadian time, on the other hand, the flow of our day as the sun broke and moved overhead before waning to dusk and dissolving to dark, became acute. The forest had its own arcs of waking and resting, the diurnal and nocturnal forces swelling contrapuntally, and I began to anticipate these orchestral shifts with little forethought, the same nonchalance you'd feel in your own neighborhood if car alarms went off predictably at two A.M., or lawn mowers roared punctually to life at ten on a Saturday.

A small plastic three-ring binder with laminated handwritten pages contained recipes and cooking instructions for one-pot dinners like soup, chili, beans and rice, and the plastic crate that served as the kitchen cupboard came fully stocked with bay leaves, tumeric, cayenne, and other seasonings in little plastic jars.

Over the weeks and months the tree had been occupied, the collective presence had thought of everything, as far as I could tell.

The first evening, lacking confidence, we watched Mole cook, who had traversed the lines to join us for dinner. He put together an easy soup with some chicken bouillon cubes, herbs, and dried pasta. The next day, to surprise him, we started a more complicated Cajun red beans and rice recipe from the binder, putting the beans to soak right after breakfast. The smells wafting up through the branches must have confused the thrushes and squirrels rustling about. We saw how quickly we could tame them if we wanted to, bringing them into our little routines, and though my impulse was to make a connection with them instead of thwart one, we tried to practice Mole's abruptness with the animals, so that they would retain a healthy wariness of us.

We washed our faces in the water from the rain catch, swept our platform several times a day with a straw broom. We didn't bathe and didn't feel dirty. When we peed off the edge of the platform, it was surprisingly unembarrassing—Neil's stream a golden arc, my more humble approach to grasp a couple of rope handholds and squat over a gap in the back of the platform designed for the purpose. Our waste fell to a shallow latrine pit below that would get shoveled over by whoever was on the ground next.

Our time in the tree passed in an easy domesticity that had nothing to do with my anxieties on the ground about lapsing into the caretaking role. I felt marooned with him in a lovely way, everything elemental and natural, no static from anyone else's expectations. I thought it would be easy to go on like this forever.

Mole spent about half of every day on our platform, and one time Neil rigged himself up to traverse the lines and visit him. I felt no need to leave our tree. The time when Neil was gone for a couple of hours, I luxuriated in the quiet, curled up with a book but mostly staring into the green canopy, still marveling that I had come to be here. It was then that I decided to call my mother. We hadn't spoken for a week now, and I knew she'd be fretting. But when I turned the phone on, the little icon of the receiver was overruled by the circle with a line through it, as if phoning home had been outlawed, like smoking in a public building.

I had known there was a chance I wouldn't get a signal, but being so definitively out of touch was unsettling. The platform was equipped with one-half of a set of walkie-talkies, should we need to alert our ground crew of any problems. But those didn't connect me to the wider world. When I discovered that I *couldn't* call my mother, I started to want to, not only to share what was here (if she'd hear it, if she was able to), but to alleviate her worry. Part of our empathy was my knowing exactly how long an absence or silence she could bear, and I wasn't interested in torturing her. She'd always cultivated a blitheness when shipping me off for a couple weeks of summer camp or even a nine-week exchange program I did in high school, lodging with a Belgian family and practicing my French. True, she'd flown to Brussels midway through my stay to steal me away for a Paris weekend, while other parents had had the stamina to make it through the entire term without showing their faces. I'd always felt that she'd practiced our separations like a kind of discipline, with the sort of determination and focus other mothers might bring to a meditation or fitness program. She sent me off with good cheer and a brightness that was meant to convey that while I was gone she would be indulging in lots of dinners out with colleagues and fundraising galas and political events. She never made me feel that I shouldn't leave her. This parting had been different, though, unbounded by academic outlines, unbuffered by programmatic safety nets. Of course, I was coming back to Wellesley in the fall, she assumed, and I'd never denied. Yet how untethered it felt to be here, and how real this was and dreamlike Wellesley seemed, conjured from this perspective. I think she knew it, too, that what I'd be doing and the people I'd be mixing with would make my world at home seem vaporous and thin and perhaps too far to reach back to.

She must have known; hadn't she done those years in the Peace Corps? And though she'd had the touchstones of official U.S. agencies regulating her stay, wouldn't she have felt something like the *permanence* of her situation when she was in the Congolese village? It had been years since I'd seen those ambering slides, but I remembered the Ginnie in them as difficult to recognize at times, a stringy leanness to her in baggy khakis and T-shirts, her hair grown out in waves and pulled severely back in a ponytail that made her face almost skull-like in its protruding cheekbones and long jaw, eye sockets hollowed by the shade of the straw hat she wore. In other shots she came more into focus as the mother I knew, her face maternally soft when holding an African child on her knee, her body a protective curve as she read him a book. I knew she'd slept on a cot in a tin-roofed dormitory, eaten the same mashed plantains and yams as the villagers, and endured fantastic heat. Ginnie had successfully made the transition back to designer clothes and restaurant meals and 300-thread-count linens, but it was a transition made before my time, and I wondered now if it was ever a transition she considered not making, or one that, imagined from Africa, seemed incredible to her.

She'd often told me stories about that time, the details having become so familiar I could narrate them as if they belonged to me, and did, in a piece of fiction that had impressed my creative writing teacher at Wellesley. It was work I would never be able to show my mother, stolen as it was from her memories. Some of the material literally *was* pilfered—drawn not from the stories she'd chosen to share, but from entries in a travel journal she kept with some old letters in a desk drawer. I knew about the drawer, it was where she kept the slides from Africa, and one afternoon when I'd had the condo to myself I'd rifled it for material that might be useful to my writing project.

When her mother had died suddenly of a stroke during her second year in the Congo, Ginnie had been summoned home for the funeral. The outlines of the story were family lore: the telegram arriving at the village two days after her mother's death, the hastily arranged ride to the train station, Ginnie the only *mundele* on the platform, the only white, among the bright butterflies of the women draped in their green and yellow *paignes*. Reading the journal, it was all suddenly vivid. I copied out the foreign words from her own writing, fingered the stub from the CFCO—Chemin de Fer Congo-Océan—my heart beating from the larcenous research the way hers must have on that lurching afternoon journey as she anticipated all the typical calamities preventing her from reaching Pointe-Noire and her flight home. But there had been no tree fallen across the tracks, no shrieking malfunction, and so she'd arrived at the hotel to phone Boston, finally reaching her father after several tries. He'd been out making arrangements, picking a stone, a lovely piece of silvery granite. What did she think of the epitaph? *Rose Murdock Prince, Beloved Wife and Mother,* followed by some lines from Dickinson, Rose's favorite poet: *Then—eddies—like a Rose—away / Upon vermilion wheels—.*

Ginnie's flight wasn't until morning; she'd spent the evening drinking in the hotel bar. Tucked into the journal's pages was a cheaply colored postcard of the Hotel Angleterre, and I pictured her sitting there among its grand colonial appointments: the slowly turning fans, mahogany shutters, polished marble floors. I watched her get picked up by the polite businessman from Germany, saw them leave the bar together for the hotel dining room, understood what a relief it would be to let someone order the meal, taste the wine, take care of everything. He'd made no secret of the wife in Köln, and that was fine, for it was only this one night that she needed him to lead her upstairs to a bed with ironed sheets, undress her, take his pleasure from her, displaying a full range of tenderness and gratitude. His weight was a good thing; she wanted an anchor to earth. She didn't tell him much about herself. She resented nothing about him and was glad that someone had seemed to require something specific from her at that moment. Ginnie had written in her journal that she'd slipped away shortly after he rolled to his own side, snoring. I'd added to my story that she'd used his towels to wipe between her legs, though the condom had prevented his fluids from entering her, and then found on his washbasin a bar of soap whose fragrance had been mixed into his pale scent. In his open toilet case she'd found two more cakes of it—linden—and she helped herself to a bar, wrapped in glossy white paper printed with German. Then—we'd both written—she'd dressed quietly and gone down to her own small room, where she vomited repeatedly into the toilet.

She'd never used the soap and kept it in the bottom drawer of her dresser at home. I'd come across it as a child when rummaging for something and asked her about the strange words on the label. She'd taken it out of my hands too quickly for it to be only soap, and said never mind, we didn't need to use that bar, we had others.

After the funeral—a black dress borrowed from Rose's perfumed closet, uncomfortable pumps sheathed around her feet whose seams were still etched with red village dust, despite soaking—my mother had returned to her posting to resume alphabet letters and primers with her children. She became attached to one seven-year-old in particular, a boy who boarded at the school and had lost his own mother the year before in childbirth. Henri brought her unusual stones and honeysuckle blossoms, and I think it was he who was in the picture with my mother, his head nuzzled against her side. She wrote that he guided her through the hidden paths under the parasoleil trees, where you could walk in a downpour and stay perfectly dry. He showed her how to make bitterleaf soup, visited with tamarind juice on a day when she was absent from school because of fever. There were drawings of stick figures I took to be the two of them together, all of them signed *love*. A carefully block-printed note saying that if she would only send a ticket he would come to stay with her in America.

Was I jealous of all this when I came across it, evidence of my mother's first child? I couldn't be; couldn't begrudge her this source of pure, unstinted affection after I had unfolded and finished reading Grandmother Rose's brisk weekly letters typed on tissue-thin airmail pages. News of classmates, neighbors, Grandfather's cases, Rose's charity work. Where had it said that Rose couldn't bear for Ginnie to be so far from her? She had directed her daughter to take care of herself, stay out of the sun, eat properly. Was it there? She had noted that Ginnie was doing important work. There? My own mother's raw longing seeped through the messages she left on the cell phone, though I knew she tried hard to avoid being maudlin. *Surely* in Rose's bulletins there was some small shred of emotion buried somewhere where my mother would be able to discover it, though it seemed unlikely to be tucked in the reference to tuning the piano, or coded between the listed items of what was blooming in the garden.

Then Rose had died, all that primness bursting free in a stroke, a blown artery pinwheeling like fireworks, like *vermilion wheels* carrying her forth to some permanent granite distance.

Where had that left my mother, in her equatorial heat, with her little motherless friend? Had she ever thought about choosing a different sort of life than the one she returned to? The one she ended up living?

There was plenty of time to talk about it when I got back, if she would, if she wouldn't preface it all by reminding me how legitimate agencies had sanctioned her efforts, in contrast to mine. Then I wouldn't have to remind her that the Peace Corps had created, according to my Poli Sci professor, the inroads and infrastructure for the multinational corporations and destabilizing modernizations of the third world that had followed. It was funny how I could follow almost any train of thought pertaining to Ginnie and arrive at some kind of virtual argument with her.

After a few lazy afternoons playing hearts together, eating dinner and smoking a joint after, then watching the stars encrust the sky like a coating of sugar, I felt Mole becoming our friend. Unlike some of the others, he lacked sanctimoniousness, and didn't show qualms about revealing parts of his past. Not that he was garrulous. One of the things he did best was sitting in silence for long unpunctuated stretches. But once during a meal when I ventured a question about his logging days, he was unexpectedly forthcoming.

"I just got to feeling what a shame it was, all that land ruined, and how I was playing a big part in it. A lot of guys never thought twice about it, their idea of getting out in nature was snowmobiling or four-wheeling through their own clearcuts. Then one day I was ordered to cut close in an area with tree-sitters, make the trees fall alongside them, get them to panic and come down."

He spooned up the last of the chili we'd made that day. Despite his dirty hands and fingernails (I glanced down—mine were now the same), he had a tidy air, neatly avoiding his beard and mustache with every bite. He wore a wool watch cap pulled down low to his eyebrows.

"I couldn't do it." He said this matter-of-factly, betraying no internal struggle or bitterness. "I knew it would be too dangerous for the sitters, and I was one of the best cutters, most accurate. I told my foreman I wouldn't do it and that no one else had the skills to, besides me. Told him I didn't want any deaths on my conscience."

"What'd he say?"

"Said to collect my gear and notify the office where to send my last check. Unless I wanted to change my mind."

"And you didn't," I said.

He shook his head.

"And then you joined the movement?"

"Not right away. The forest people still looked a little strange to me." He grinned, showing small, surprisingly even teeth. "Took me a while to get over that."

I loved him for admitting it. Hadn't I thought the same? It was as if all the toxin-free air they breathed and vegan food they ate had worn away too many edges. Their unshaved gentleness, their own particular brand of conformity in their tie-dyes and Indian cottons or Guatemalan wools, seemed too pious, and somehow— I don't know—witless. Not as in stupid, but as in smilingly humorless, without irony or surprising jests of thought.

"But you did."

"Yeah, I drove out to see a protest at a timber sale—one I'd have been working at if I'd stayed with the company—mostly out of curiosity. I saw the police hustling off the journalists—you know, getting a little rough with their cameras—pushing some teenagers around, handcuffing one girl who'd locked herself to a bulldozer with her bicycle lock."

"And that did it for you?"

"Well"—Mole pointed questioningly to the last spoonful of chili in the pot and, when we shook our heads, helped himself— "I'd always felt bad about some of the cutting. Not all—I mean, it's unrealistic to expect this country to give up its wood products— but the old growth. No need to take it, no need at all. Pure company greed. More board feet of lumber in one old-growth tree than in half a dozen second-growth trees. It's no mystery why they don't want to give it up without a fight."

Mole finished the last of his dinner and sat back, grooming the corners of his mouth with a quick swipe of his hand.

"How long had you been logging?" Neil asked.

"Since high school," Mole said. "That'd make it ten or more years."

"So you knew the operations inside and out."

"Yup." Mole grinned. "I had some ideas for the protesters when I started coming around. They didn't believe me at first, thought I was a spy for the company. I said, if I was a spy, why would I tell you right out that I was a logger? Why wouldn't I come dressed in one of those LEGALIZE HEMP T-shirts? They weren't convinced until I got arrested."

"What'd you do to get arrested?"

"Something small. Trespassing charge. I wouldn't have been much help locked away."

I realized that Mole had engineered his first arrest to establish his credentials, and had again the uneasy notion that Neil might not be beyond doing the same. There was his infatuation with Thoreau, the tidbits he'd read aloud to me our first day in the tree—"It is not desirable to cultivate a respect for the law, so much as for the right"—and his heartfelt admiration of Henry in jail, while the morally inferior Waldo stood on the free side of the bars.

After supper Mole produced a baggie of dope from his shirt pocket and proceeded to roll a professionally thin and smooth joint. A few drops of rain had quickened into a steady fall, so Neil unfurled our tarp, tying its corners to branches. In the lull of twilight time the forest was quiet, so all we heard was the regular tapping of rain on our plastic roof and the faint, intermittent sizzle of the joint as Mole inhaled, then passed it to Neil, who in turn passed it to me. You wouldn't think that, on a perch so high, in a place whose location I could only vaguely pinpoint, all the while knowing myself to be in multiple violations of the law, I could have felt so safe. But whether it was the sweet smoke curling around us like a pet, or being in company I loved, or the cool, rain-drummed night, I felt a sense of well-being possess my entire self like a purring. Neil sat up against the trunk of our massive tree and I leaned against him, my head pillowed on his stomach. Mole stretched out on his side, separated from us by a few feet. We took turns telling stories, or Mole and Neil did, as I listened, feeling as if I were floating above them, beneficent and calm.

"Folks, I think I'm gonna have to crash here for the night," Mole said lazily, the tip of our second shared joint a small firefly that flared briefly and made its way over to us.

"Of course you will," I said, because Neil was occupied with holding in his smoke. "A slumber party."

Neil released his breath slowly, his abdomen deflating under me. A funny word, *abdomen*. It cracked me up.

"*Head, and thorax, ab-do-men, ab-do-men*," I sang softly, a ditty that suddenly suggested itself from a toddler repertoire archived deep within my synapses. It was odd, the little doors of the brain that could suddenly spring open. Like an Advent calendar, toy thoughts stored behind each one.

"*Head, and thorax, ab-do-men, ab-do-men*," I continued to the tune of "Head and Shoulders Knees and Toes."

"Maybe you've had enough," Neil said, the joint suspended above me.

I shook my head and took it from him, inhaled and held the smoke bottled up inside me like a genie, suppressing the urge to cough.

"The Ant Lady taught it to us," I explained after exhaling, handing the joint back to Mole. "She brought her giant model of the ant and taught us to sing the parts along with her."

"The Ant Lady?" Mole asked. "Am I missing something?"

"No, you're not missing anything," I said. "Unless the Ant Lady never came to visit your preschool. Then you missed."

"Preschool," Mole snorted. "Who went to preschool?"

"Who remembers it if they did?" Neil asked.

"She brought us paper headbands with pipe-cleaner feelers."

"Antennae," Neil corrected absently.

"It's okay to say feelers," I admonished him gently. "She dipped cotton balls in either peppermint or lemon extract and attached them to the ends of our feelers. I was a lemon ant. Then we went around sniffing each other's feelers, finding our family."

"Sounds kinky," Mole said.

"No, it wasn't," I said dreamily. "It wasn't kinky a bit."

Mole clipped the nubbin that was left of the joint to a roach and offered it to Neil.

"No, you go ahead," he said.

He moved his hand to me and I shook my head as well. "All yours."

A meditative silence fell as we watched the glow of Mole's last tokes.

"Actually, ants are really interesting," Neil said. "When I was ten I got one of those plastic ant keepers for my birthday. You had to send in a coupon for the actual ants."

"My mother never liked bugs in the house," I said. "Not that I recall ever asking for any."

"They came in a glass test tube. Packed together and swarming all over each other's bodies like they were angry."

"Well, yeah," I said. "Wouldn't you be?"

Mole was quiet, listening, or maybe dozing off, it was too dark to see his eyes. I fell silent, too, and Neil began filling the emptiness with the story of his ants—his life, really, as I came to understand it in my heightened state of perception. His words fell directly into my brain like rain, each one a transparent globe of meaning, everything making perfect sense and connecting itself effortlessly to every other thought I'd ever had. *Of course,* I remember thinking. *That's exactly why this exact moment exists.*

And then I kept his story, pressing it in memory like a corsage, because it was his and he'd entrusted it to me.

THE STORY OF THE LAST ANT
Or, A True History of Neil's Alienation
Or, Reasons Why Civilization Is Doomed

Refrigerate tube, the instructions had said, *until your ants are stunned.* Sure enough, the chilled ants had been still and compliant as Neil shook them out of their tube and into the habitat he had prepared. Slowly they'd warmed and come to life and adjusted to the fact that they were back in sand, not their original sand in Arizona, from where the padded envelope had been shipped, but sand Neil had carefully poured out of the plastic bag that came with the kit. He'd moistened it with spring water before packing it loosely into the dome-shaped plastic viewer, which came complete with small molded houses and cars.

The ants had thrived in their new, protected world. They'd seemed genuinely grateful for the sweetened water Neil dripped into their village "pond," coming in groups to drink and socialize. They'd gone dutifully to work after their liquid refreshment, carrying the sand a grain at a time down the various openings the manufacturer had provided, laying tunnels in the appointed places, creating ever more elaborate arterial intersections and connecting ramps. At first they'd seemed bent on erasing the little Monopoly-sized houses on the plastic oak-lined streets by methodically burying them, until Neil realized that they were actually enshrining them, claiming them for their own in their underground engineering masterpiece.

He'd wondered what the ants would do when they'd tunneled as much as they could in their limited space, but as their network of passages had become increasingly lacelike, he'd seen them occupied with ever-increasing amounts of repair and renovation, the net effect being that they maintained full employment while GNP continued to expand at a robust rate, an impressive display of dedication to the notion of progress given the finity of their grains of sand.

Eventually they'd died, of course, but not of any poisoned ecosystem. Neil had been too conscientious a keeper to permit rotting morsels of grapes to foul their air or to allow the humidity to veer in the direction of either desert or rain forest. He'd made sure his ants lived in a temperate, even climate, away from the heat-magnifying effect of his bedroom window. What killed them, one at a time, was age, the simple expiration of their nine-or-so-month life span as stated in the brochure, and since his ants were all sterile workers, there would be no successive generation to take their place unless he sent a new order form to the supplier in Arizona.

Each ant had been buried by the others, carried up to the surface of the dome from whatever tunnel it had collapsed in after laying a last grain. The colony had zoned the heart of town for the cemetery, a decent reach from the watering hole but prominently central. It soon became the largest feature of the village. Each deceased worker had been laid on top of the pile—Neil had been reminded of the "viewing hours" during which he'd gone with his family to have a final look at his waxy, rosy grandfather—before other workers visited, leaving behind a grain of sand until the corpse had been successfully buried and the monument the ants were building to their own mortality had risen a degree higher.

Neil had observed carefully to see what would become of the final ant, whether it would suffer ignominious exposure in death, stranded in some far alley, or if it understood its lastness and would somehow provide for its own rites and ceremony. It survived stubbornly past all predictions of the brochure, ten months, eleven, not taking retirement or even holiday, but going to work day after day, making unnecessary modifications in the tunnel branches, maintaining roadways only it would travel. Finally, impatiently, Neil unscrewed the roof of the dome and removed the last ant into a tupperware container, not even bothering to stun it first with a few minutes in the refrigerator.

He'd told himself he was doing the ant a favor, taking it for a last outing in the world, under real sky and sun and letting it have a final taste of the authentic. But, even at ten, he'd suspected his own perversity, the cruelty of undoing all the systems and rituals the ant had in place. He wasn't pretending that the ant's capabilities were larger than they were, that its neural functioning was sophisticated enough to experience wonder or joy, release or

relief. He'd known the ant was a social insect and that, as sole sur-
vivor, it was presently lost, whether trapped in the plastic dome
or stranded on his driveway on Arcadia Street. It was his own
understanding of the ant's predicament he hadn't been able to tol-
erate a moment longer. He'd had to admit that, after the initial
excitement of setting up the colony, his ants had depressed him.
They'd understood tribal behavior better than he ever had, and
they'd seemed not only perfectly content with the artificial world
he'd presented them with, but, given their animation at the watering hole, their zeal for improvements, delighted with it.

Neil had watched the ant zig and zag on the cement, antennae
working furiously, then, his attention momentarily drawn away by
something—maybe the tracing of a jet or the bell of an ice-cream
truck—he'd looked down to find the ant missing. Vanished. There
were many cracks it could have disappeared into for shelter, and
he'd waited for it to come barreling out again, disoriented and panicky. He'd planned, after giving it this field trip, to return it to the
dome where it could live out its remaining days in unpredated
peace, repairing bridges to its heart's content. But, though Neil
waited and watched for many minutes, his last ant never returned.

The ant might have been attacked immediately by a soldier ant
from a driveway colony—such were the aggressions of tribes—or
it might have found a dark crevice to cower in, shocked into dor-
mancy by the vastness of life outside the dome. Neil had been
disappointed that he'd not been able to observe the denouement
of the little civilization he'd played God to. It had felt like his
right to witness the end, since he'd engineered the beginning, and
since he'd been the mysterious hand bearing the dropper of sug-
ared water every seventh day.

Neil believed in no comparable deity for mankind, no rescue in the shape of a miraculous hand bearing down. Humanity, compelled by some wiring in the evolutionary software to pile up bricks and then swing the wrecking balls to knock them down again, was doomed to the pleasure and destruction of its own industry. It was too late to slow it down—people *liked* tunneling their way from their houses (synthetically sided and floored and roofed) through their attached garages to their sealed capsules of automobiles to drive their ordained daily routes. They *liked* nosing their steel-sided SUVs into the darkness of parking garages exited by way of elevators directly into climate-controlled malls or office buildings. It was *entirely okay* with most people to not touch the weather, to not be dampened by rain or exposed to sun (the irony being that they intended to use a portion of their economic gain, after consumption, to purchase a unit of Vacation Leisure in a setting that would convincingly simulate or even provide limited direct contact with these very same natural elements).

He feared it was too late even for those well-meaning folk who still managed to use their legs to walk places, who still gardened, patronized mass transit, recycled their trash, and refused to waste water resources on chemically farmed plots of lawn. Because those hopeful souls wouldn't, in the end, opt out. They were too well behaved; they put too much stock in process, in fiascos like environmental summits and Kyoto accords which the bloated, drugged, industrialized nations of the world, America chief among them, would always subvert. *Process* meant the next grain of sand futilely piled on the last grain, even if the structure was collapsing from within.

It might be too late, but Neil was not inherently a fatalist, or even a pessimist. He no longer believed in petitions or legislation, dissertations or seminars, or humanity's spontaneous renunciation of things like a convenient disposable plastic container for each day's Lunchable. But he did believe in the power of shock and disruption. He'd come to understand that a well-placed explosion could get the herd's attention, make journalists ask interesting questions, and shine the spotlight of truth on destructive and deceitful corporate interests. It didn't matter if he and the others were discredited by the law-abiding public with every story on the evening news about arson in a university lab, computers crashing at government offices, swarms of minks liberated from their cages. Society's tut-tuts meant nothing. What mattered was that the antlike public receive a tiny blip in its obedient mass consciousness; that disobedience be seen as a possibility, and that change—genuine, violent change—be offered as an option available to all.

Activists might have to be sacrificed to these goals, and, his arms tightening around me, Neil announced that he was prepared to be one of them. He said he saw himself as fully equipped for the responsibilities of martyrdom: What had all that graduate research and writing prepared him for if not an effective articulation of the issues? He told me my mother was correct, in a limited way. He could be a spokesperson, but not from within the system. To speak from within was to condone the system, be part of it.

Neil wound down to silence then—I felt him loosen his hold on me, heard his even breaths deepen to a soft snore as he drifted off—but I remained trapped awake inside his words (for what had begun as a bedtime story had ended as a manifesto, its hard certainties softened only by the invisible rustlings of the flying squirrels). I tried to use my new, pot-induced nimbus of inner light to weigh my commitment to this action. Was I along for the ride, or was I really here, one of them? The spotted owls were emblematic of it, the mysterious plenti-tude beyond our cities and subdivisions. Mole had taught us to listen for the barking cries of the nesting pair a few hundred feet distant, heard but not yet seen, and their baby who was just learn-ing to hoot.

I listened now, the only one awake, not hearing the owls but feeling possessive of the darkness, its lush embrace of me and the animals. In the dark I felt momentarily freed from all the human claims on my loyalty, those importuning hands on my wrist. Eventually I'd have to choose.

The next morning we were barely awake and lighting our stove for tea and oatmeal when we heard them.

"Hey, shitheads," a voice called through a bullhorn. I froze, icy beneath my wool sweater. It was impossible to tell from which direction the voice came. It was just a bellowing forth as if a malicious, foulmouthed god had been loosed on us.

"Get ready to be pulled down from there, assholes," the voice said.

Neil had the binoculars out, scanning around the platform.

"That's right, you cocksuckers. You can either climb down yourselves like good little apes, or we'll come get you. If we have to climb all the way up all that good lumber to get you, we're gonna be pissed."

"That's not the police," I said, paralyzed where I sat, the container of oatmeal in my hand.

Mole rubbed his eyes and shook his head. "Nah. Company goons. They're just trying to rattle us."

They shouted obscenities and threats at us for twenty minutes before they finally seemed to tire of the sound of their own voices. After a short silence we heard the whine of a buzz saw starting up and ripping through a trunk, followed by a cracking and splintering, and then a muffled fall. Mole pointed to the sudden animation of some branches a few hundred yards away where the tree must have toppled against it, but he never did see the man or men, how many of them there might have been. I didn't know if they had a view of us or not. I thought not, especially as I'd backed away from the platform's edge. I wasn't about to let them see the fear on my face.

"Just getting warmed up, motherfuckers! Just getting ready to come after that pretty little pile of wood you're squatting in! Maybe we won't bother climbing it first to pull you out. Maybe we'll just start cutting. See you soon, assholes! Can't wait!"

My limbs jangled in the aftermath of their noise, as if some vibration from their saws had penetrated my body and remained active there. It was adrenaline, suddenly changing its effect from paralysis to an almost unbearable surfeit of strength. For the first time since being on the platform I felt confined, like an animal in a cage, except in a cage I would be able to pace to spend down my energy, and here we couldn't even do that.

"Those creeps!" I burst out. "How can they do that?"

Neil looked outwardly calm, but his jaw was tight and a thin muscle jumped in his neck. I'd never seen him really angry before.

"I'd love to see them try it," he said quietly, and I had visions of Neil engaged in hand-to-hand combat with some logger halfway up a tree. Surreal as it seemed, I didn't doubt that it could happen, and I believed him when he said he'd relish it. I'd almost relish it myself.

"They're making empty threats," Mole said, patting my forearm. "Completely empty."

"You mean they're not coming to cut?"

"Oh, they'll come cut if they can," he said. "But no one is going to climb up here and pull you out of the tree."

"How do you know?" I demanded. During the stream of profanities I'd wondered if they knew a woman was up here, and if they would have switched to "cunt" and "bitch" if they'd known.

"Loggers don't climb trees. They're beer-swilling guys who are more comfortable with machines than athletics. The company would have to hire a climber—not cheap. And not safe, either, for the climber. Imagine how hard it would be to pull someone off a platform and stay stable yourself. Who wants that kind of work?" He shook his head, smiling reassuringly at me. "Intimidation tactics, pure and simple."

"You mean they're just going to leave us alone?" I asked.

"Not exactly. They could start cutting around us. It's not too pleasant sitting up in a tree listening to buzz saws all day. They'll blast music at us, or shine lights at night, or do more of what they just did—ugly language, threats."

"Try to psyche us down," said Neil tensely.

"My guess is that they're the advance guys and that we might not have more visitors for a while." Mole commandeered the walkie-talkie and checked in with Mudman, who crackled back in hard-to-understand replies that Mole pressed to his ear. When he was finished, he looked at us and said, "Mudman thinks it might be time for a shift change tomorrow."

Relief flooded me, but Neil said, "Wait a minute, we're not scared to take these guys on." I shot him a look.

"It's not about you," Mole said. "There's going to be plenty for you to do. This is standard procedure, try and keep everyone rotated while we still can. You're not being treated differently."

Neil shook his head. "It feels personal now."

Mole held his eyes. "That's a good reason to come down and do something else. There's a kind of anger that helps and a kind that gets in the way. You're no good to us if you do something stupid and get hurt."

"What about you? Are you coming down?"

"Sure. I've got another project in mind on the ground. Maybe you can help."

At this Neil relented, and I finally took a breath. I heard my mother cheering wildly from somewhere in Boston. While I didn't want to be seen as cowardly, I also didn't look forward to listening to the abuse again. They'd threatened to cut—had, in fact, cut something, and Mole himself had said that felling trees around the sitters was dangerous. Was it selfish to love my one little life and want to cling to it? Compared to death or injury at the hands of the company, arrest suddenly seemed a petty thing, something lawyers like my mother could fix up in an afternoon's work. My perspective had subtly shifted after the goons' visit. I don't know if that was the morning I was "radicalized," in the parlance of the movement, or if the incident had just planted one of several seeds that would germinate over the next days and weeks. I did know rage suddenly played a role in what I believed. I had met the enemy.

11

"Largely peaceful." I grinned at Starling when I was on the ground again. The machines had not come within sight of us on the last day, nor had the goons returned. I'd begun to relax again, even wishing that our stay in the trees could go on for weeks. Lowering myself down in those jerky, swinging bounces, I'd had time to feel an impossible inverse gravitational pull—a force willing me back up to the nest where we'd sheltered next to the dense heartwood of the tree, rather than down to the safe and ordinary ground.

Not that I wasn't glad to move around again now, get my body moving. Starling and I fell behind the others a bit, talking.

"There's a court date coming up," she said. "If our lawyers get the restraining order, we won't be seeing them for a while."

"You mean you can stop them?" I said incredulously.

"Oh, now and then we can delay them."

"And that's enough?"

She made a face and I thought again of Sara. Even the way of wrinkling the nose was the same. I wanted to know Starling's name, her real one, because it didn't seem like we could become friends without knowing who each other really was. Maybe sometime she'd tell me. Or maybe the idea was not to become friends. Just strangers working efficiently together.

"It's never enough, because too much damage has been done already. Every time there's a new clearcut the ecology changes permanently."

"But this particular court date. You think there's a chance?"

"There's actually an excellent chance of getting the new restraining order, because Wainwright Timber is in violation of the law, and we can prove it. We've got video of them taking trees outside the permit zone, of them felling a tagged old-growth fir because it was where they wanted their road to go."

"That's great."

Starling looked at me with the measured smile you'd bestow on a child who hadn't grasped the lesson but was trying.

"It's great as long as someone is out here, watching and filming their every move. It's a big forest and as soon as no one's looking they'll do what they want."

"But we are watching."

"Yeah. Right now." She pressed her lips together and fell silent and I didn't have anything to say in return. Her flat tone killed my optimism, made me feel silly for having it in the first place. I'd been up in one tree for a few days. How was that going to permanently help anything when there were corporate interests with plenty of lawyers and clear economic motives? All they needed was a long-term strategy. I began to see the dangers of caring about this; every day of involvement would make it harder and harder to walk away. The amount of witness and protest and civil disobedience necessary to change the course of government or business—either one, but especially the two hand-in-hand—was immense. There would be no closure to it, no finishing a tree-sit and so finishing a job. If I didn't keep myself apart, it would begin to feel like a mission, a choice that was no choice.

But already I wasn't apart. When we returned to the circle I was even glad to see Squirrel, the flat-faced girl, as she laid out the dinner and smiled at me shyly. Every one of them had also put himself or herself in danger. There was no reward to it, no prize at the end or seeing your picture in the newspaper with a caption about your efforts. There were only costs: If your picture made the paper it would be bad news. If you were here in the woods that meant you weren't finishing school or earning money or having a family or traveling for pleasure or doing the work that mattered only to you, personally.

Although, I reminded myself, this *was* Neil's work. I'd never seen him so animated. His eyes were bright and he grinned at everyone as he accepted congratulations and talked about what it felt like to be in the tree. People were smiling indulgently at him as they listened. They weren't cutting him off or reminding him that they'd done it. They were taking pleasure in his pleasure.

I was getting the last of my soup up with a crust of bread—still hungry, but feeling that it wouldn't be good form to go back for more—when Spiderman sat down beside me on the ground, letting his long legs stretch out in front of him.

"You did good," he said.

I looked at him, lifting my brows.

"You did," he said. He had a nice smile when he let himself. Snaggled teeth that had needed orthodontia and didn't get it, but nice. I wondered what made him seem so angry most of the time, and why he was giving me a break now.

"Well, thanks," I said. "I don't think I would have made it up the tree if you hadn't coached me out of my panic."

"Probably not."

I chose not to be annoyed. "How'd you get to be such a climber?"

He cocked his head, and I saw that his nose was crooked—the heavy mustache drew attention away from both the nose and the teeth. Crooked nose, crooked teeth. I suddenly wondered if those thin legs were crooked, too.

"This for your journal?" he said.

"Oh, no," I said. "I'd actually like to write it up and publish it. Maybe send a copy to the FBI. Post it on a website."

He chuckled. "Army is how."

I nodded. I'd never known anyone who had been in the army except friends of my grandfather's who had all sorts of decorations for World War II. I didn't want the exchange to die between us, but I wondered how to keep it going without resorting to a personal line of questioning.

"How'd you get from the army to here?" I asked. "If it's not classified."

He shrugged. "Just kicked around a little, here and there."

"I don't know how anyone is supposed to have a conversation around here," I said, letting the irritation into my voice.

"We're having a conversation," he said.

"Is that what you'd call it?"

He raised his eyebrows at me. "Why're you always so sassy?"

I rolled my eyes and leaned back against the log, looking away from him into the fire.

"It's not very interesting how I got here is all."

"Uh-huh."

"My, my," he said, clucking his tongue.

"Look, I'm not being hostile," I said preemptively, because I had the feeling that the next thing he was going to say was that I was the bitchiest woman—no, he'd say *girl*—he'd ever met in the movement.

"That's okay," he said. "Be hostile. Don't hurt me none."

"Let's just drop it."

"It's dropped," he said, shrugging again and gathering his legs under him in preparation to stand up.

I wanted him to wait, to sit back down and keep me company some more, but I didn't know anything to say to make him stay. Across the campsite Neil was regaling Coot with something or other, I couldn't hear the words, could only read the vivid hand motions and the enthusiastic inflections of his voice that were carried over to me every now and then in a gust of laughter.

Everyone seemed high on nerves and excitement now that the other side had actively engaged us. The elves had also spied the mechanics tinkering with the sabotaged machines and gleefully reported that they hadn't been able to get them running. Operations were definitely hampered.

"Are they just going to stand for that?" I asked Starling as I helped her wash up the soup kettle and stow the supplies. She didn't need help, but I felt self-conscious and alone sitting against my log, my elation ebbing away after the encounter with Spiderman. I wanted female company, and made my way over to Starling's comfortingly solid figure in overalls.

"Oh, in the long run I'm sure they'll get nastier and nastier. I'd guess they don't want to do anything too outrageous before the court date next week. Their lawyers will be able to point to the crimes committed against them and, of course, they'll deny cutting outside of the permit zone."

"But they can't, right? I mean, you've got the video?"

"Yeah, we've got the video. But all it means is that at best they'll be stopped for a while. And even if they stay within the cutting zone that's not a good thing, either. Lobbyists are trying to get more land under protection, but that will come too little, too late."

"How can you stand to keep doing it?" I asked her. We had finished putting things back in the canvas supply bags and had strung them up above ground level. Now we were just leaning back against a tree trunk, sipping leftover tea from a thermos. "You sound so depressed by it all, so certain it's going to all be for nothing."

"It might be," she agreed. "But how can anybody *not* do it? That's what I want to know. Imagine if everyone cared enough to just come out and stand side by side at the entrance to a logging project. Middle-class people, everyone. Shoulder to shoulder, so they couldn't break through without hurting someone. Picture the media attention that would bring, the wake-up call to legislators."

I smiled at her encouragingly, wanting her to talk more, wanting to feel some hopefulness.

"It won't happen, of course. As long as they leave some recreation areas, some nicely groomed hiking trails and inspirational overlooks that face away from the clearcuts, people won't care. Even the ones that claim to love wilderness are more interested in getting electricity and roads into the back country so they can have a lakefront cabin somewhere, complete with DVD player and cappuccino maker and a parking space for the SUV."

I made a face. "Now I'm depressed."

She smiled and patted my knee. "You should be. We all should be. Then we'll work harder. Convince more people. And if we don't. . . ." She shook her head. "It's nice being out here, isn't it? Having it?"

"I almost can't imagine anything else right now. I'm trying to picture my street in Boston, in the Back Bay"—I glanced sideways at her to see if her expression was gathering into disapproval, if she wanted me to keep myself wholly to myself like the rest of them did—"and I literally can't get back to the idea of pavements and sidewalks and traffic."

She hadn't frowned. "Wait until you leave and go back even to a town like Eugene," she said. "It's mind-blowing how sensitive you are to noise, how everything feels false and surreal. I call it enviro-shock instead of culture shock."

"It's like this swallows you up and becomes the truth." By *this* I meant the ever-present undervoices of the woods, its hoots and whistles, rustlings and high-pitched cries. You constantly saw the squirrels and birds, occasionally spied the deer, but you knew you were surrounded by much more than that—an entire nation of small rodents and invisibly gnawing insects, and the larger, stealthier animals. How to describe how the air and light seemed to permeate my cells, the oxygen sparkling there, my neurons relaxing away from unnatural electric light at unnatural hours. Right now the moon, smeared with seas like greasy pencil erasures, gave us just enough light to see by. As the air cooled, I wanted to retreat and burrow like an animal, find Neil and my sleeping bag and let the heavy sleep come. The pleasure of being with Starling kept me a moment more, our plastic cups of tea just about drained. One or two cooled sips I wouldn't waste, wouldn't just throw into the dirt.

"It *is* the truth, and that's how I stay sane about it all. If no one else gets it, then, well, they just don't, that's all."

Even though it was I who had first used the word *truth*, it was Starling who uttered it with the certainty that made me feel our differences. Something of my mother's temperament resided in me and wouldn't be denied. "Those capital-T truthers," she'd say dismissively, whether referring to the left or the right, or the religiously inspired. She saw the world as too jigsawed with complexity to find an absolute anywhere.

I was perhaps the one absolute in her life, the one thing she would do anything, risk anything, to protect. It was a thought that should have been comforting yet wasn't, perhaps as a result of my decisive distance from her, my growing away like a plant toward its own possession of the open elements.

12

Someone other than Shaman ferried us back to Eugene, a graduate student in math at the university who had driven up with sacks of new supplies from the food co-op. To my surprise, she was simply Cathy, rather than Larkspur or Stinkweed or Marmot. (Now more fully acquainted with my field guide, I definitely would have picked something other than the overly reverent "Emerald" if I had it to do over. Maybe something sowing homonymic confusion, like "Yew.") I began to distinguish the circles of activists, then—the shadow people in the forest, as opposed to the exposed public citizens of the town, the ones who held petitions at the Saturday Market and wrote signed letters to the editors of the *Oregonian* and the *Register-Guard*. Cathy was of the latter group. Both types are necessary, Mole asserted over morning coffee at the Vine, the vegan café where the circles met and overlapped.

"Every sympathetic group advances the cause. Even the suburban homeowner who doesn't want to look too closely at the issues out of fear he'll have to plead guilty for buying in to the new subdivision. But his conscience may trouble him just enough to drive an economy car and sign a petition, and—maybe, just maybe—send a check to one of the mainstream lobby organizations like the ONRC—"

"The . . . ?" I interrupted.

"Oregon Natural Resources Council. Or the Sierra Club, or the National Forest Protection Alliance, take your pick. The legitimate nonprofit that hires lobbyists and publishes an annual report that comes with a little donation envelope tucked inside."

I was beginning to think of Mole as the philosopher of the movement. If Starling was the den mother, and Mudman the general, and Spiderman the commando, then Mole—unlikely character that he was, logger turned forest elf—was the one who gave me a kind of ethical narrative for thinking about the whole drama.

Neil had been tucking into his tofu and vegetable scramble. We were both freshly washed from the shower at Cathy's house where we'd been lodged, though Neil had given in to the prevailing aesthetic of our new peers and decided not to shave. His stubble was darkly attractive but (literally) irritating. I, on the other hand, had defiantly shaved my legs and armpits, and now, a tad self-consciously, enjoyed rubbing my bare shins together while I stole glances at the variously furred legs of the other women in the café. No one seemed to be focusing on my legs with condemning stares, but I felt transgressive anyway.

"Well and good," Neil said, his voice gathering a little heat. "But half of those well-meant donations get eaten up by administrative costs, and the other half gets wasted on lobbying efforts that end up fostering corrupt compromises." I knew the conversation was probing a nerve with Neil, the same one my mother had tried to touch, though she didn't have the necessary influence over him to do so. But when Mole spoke benignly of the mainstream organizations, the same ones Neil would be well positioned to serve with his academic credentials, it seemed to be personally threatening to his sense of right action.

But Mole only said, "Maybe," in his characteristically mild voice, and sipped his coffee. He hadn't ordered food for himself, though the home fries were heavenly here and the coarse oatmeal bread with marionberry jam was the best I'd ever had. Such cooking didn't come for free, or even cheap, and when Mole waved away his menu I wondered if it was because he didn't have the money for a meal. No credit cards here, of course, but my roll of cash supplemented by Neil's half of the tabs on our trip out was fat and at my disposal. I'd been on the brink of offering to treat Mole and maybe should have. The fact of my money was both a comfort and a source of confusion to me. How much to act like I didn't have it, how much to spread it around at the risk of seeming patronizing? I never wanted to wish it away or renounce it, though, which confirmed my sense of myself as someone incapable of genuine self-denial.

"Maybe," Mole continued, his apparent acquiescence just a meditative pause, "but the middle class has credibility that some of the fine folks here at the Vine will never possess." He gestured to the issue of *Green Riot* I had picked up, the header that inquired, "Destroy Cities?" "You don't want to turn away the Audubon crowd, just because you might be pursuing more subterranean methods at the same time."

Mole and Neil continued to debate, while I looked around and wondered what the patrons of the sunlit Vine, presently lounging over late breakfasts, did for money. Cathy was putting us up for free while we were in town and had said to help ourselves to her cooking supplies (though I fully intended to shop for her). Apparently she was an established stop on this underground railway; she seemed to know Mole well and I'd begun to think they were lovers, he moved so familiarly in her kitchen, joked easily with her about the esoteric equations she devoted her days to.

Outside our window a white guy with Rastafarian dreadlocks had set up an easel and some acrylics and was painting a mystical vision of a rose blooming out of a sleeping woman's forehead. It was a garishly toned bit of sententiousness. A girl in a gauze skirt lounged on a bench watching him, twisting a braid with one finger while she rested her bare feet on a golden retriever. Maybe they were all students getting loan and grant checks every term. Maybe they would graduate and find themselves unwelcome at their parents' houses and gradually grow hungry enough that the plenteous body hair would be incrementally groomed back in direct proportion to the number of unanswered résumés they e-mailed out.

Or was I simply jealous because he was painting and I wasn't? My mother found it impossible to understand how I could have won the senior art prize at Briar and gone on to set myself so staunchly against painting at Wellesley. Since I so obviously did not follow her interest into law, she was constantly urging me to play to my strengths, whatever they might be, the unspoken message being that as long as I proved myself a genius in some field, I'd be bearing out the family destiny.

I had not entirely abandoned art at college, but thought of the sculpting and pottery classes I'd taken as mainly recreational. I had presented my mother with a pair of clay female nudes for her birthday, which now occupied niches of honor on the marble mantel in the Back Bay condo. The mugs and fruit bowl were in the glass-front kitchen cupboards. But there had been no drawing, none at all, until the sketching on this trip, my first excursion back to the line. Now that I was drawing again I felt the familiar anxiety that my vision was somehow paltry, a schoolgirl's vision, as tedious in my way as the Rastafarian's visions. There was a girl at Briar whose drawings were wildly, violently surreal, and another whose work had had an interesting Fauvist flatness, all vivid colors and a fetchingly skewed scale. Don't worry about a personal style yet, my teacher told me (a woman with a spiky haircut and an endless supply of black clothes, who had once showed her photo-realism regularly in New York, and then, inexplicably, didn't). Your personal commitments will come, she'd said. But what if my sense of limitation persisted? What if I remained trapped in a narrow literalness and had nothing original or interesting to say? I avoided the question by not painting.

Our breakfast plates cleared away, Neil and Mole showing no signs of winding up, I interrupted them to say I was going to wander for a bit. Neil smiled and gathered my hair off my neck as he paused briefly in his conversation. He seemed always to know what kind of touch would feel pleasant, and as the lifted hair allowed cool air across my neck I tilted my head to press my cheek against the back of his hand. I put down some money and told them I'd be back in fifteen minutes or so. We were in Eugene to help Mole with his mysterious "project," which we had yet to have explained to us. Meanwhile, I was happy to explore the town, which had only been a blur to me on our way in. As Cathy had reversed the magic of the shrinking roads, ending with the super-sized I-5 and a choice of multiple exits into Eugene, I was beginning to feel a little more confident of my bearings in this landscape. I experienced some of the enviro-shock Starling had mentioned, a disoriented and somewhat rabbity sense of being too much out in the open, but once off the major arteries, Eugene was cozy. Cathy's rented two-bedroom bungalow was tucked on a weedy square of lawn in the university district, where bicycles and pedestrians were more ubiquitous than cars. The Vine was on the other end of downtown in a funky area near the railroad tracks where converted warehouses and nineteenth-century brick buildings housed a variety of craft, book, and import shops. There was a coffeehouse on every corner in this town, almost none of them Starbucks. Each one had its own lived-in furniture and particular twist: the one with the astrology theme, the chrome urbanity of another, the Italian espresso and Tuscan pottery of a third—all within blocks of each other, all apparently finding enough customers to remain in business. When Cathy had toured us through the downtown she explained to me that in the Northwest coffee was a necessary drug to cope with the unrelenting gray and rain.

I had yet to see much rain, though it had been overcast half of the time we were in the woods. I liked it, the comforting feeling of being shielded under a warm, gray sky like a layer of homey cotton batting tucking you in. And I was already addicted to the exceptional lattes I'd been getting.

I poked through a used bookshop, drawn to a box of antique postcards of the region, especially the turn-of-the-century loggers with their brushy mustaches and thick boots, holding handsaws and posing with stiff dignity beside felled trees whose trunk diameter matched a man's height. I bought a few, not as specimens of historical villainy, but because I liked the sober pride in their faces. I could imagine doing something multimedia with them, part collage, part painting.

After my wanderings had taken me past the courthouses and city hall, the small park square, more coffeehouses seeded among the less glamorous insurance offices and unexceptional chain retail outlets, I headed the few blocks back to the Vine. Neil and Mole were waiting for me outside on the bench where the barefoot girl and her dog had lately been, and the dreadlocked artist, who had momentarily abandoned his project, leaving the easel and paint box unattended. I took advantage of his absence to get a closer look to see how truly bad the piece was. Before I turned away the painter was at my elbow, and I had to look up and be acknowledged.

"Feel free," he said. "Look all you want."

A compliment formed reflexively on my lips—because that's what you're supposed to offer when you look at someone's work—and died there.

"Do you show?" I finally mustered.

"Here and there. Bookstores, coffeehouses. I've got one in there." He gestured with his chin inside the Vine. "And I do some illustrating and advertising work. Here, take a card."

He was surprisingly well organized for a painter of mystical visions. His homemade laser-printed card advertised *Earth Arts,* and was festooned with a tree whose branches curled symmetrically aboveground to its roots below. I recognized the curling line work of the Vine's logo, transferred onto their menus and organic cotton T-shirts.

"Is that yours, too?" I pointed to the logo painted on the café's hanging wood sign. He smiled and nodded, pleased. He probably bartered a business graphic for an acupuncture session, a logo design for two weeks of vegan meals. It didn't make me any more attracted to his dreaming-woman-with-rose painting, but at least he was making art that people wanted. That was something.

Mole and Neil were rising and stretching to go. I loved our lazy morning. I liked having "business" that involved no work, projects that demanded nothing of us. The late June sunshine was balmy and inviting; I wondered if the day's agenda involved any naps or perhaps a drive to the park on the Willamette for a picnic.

"Let's go scope the site," Mole said, and I wondered if I had missed the moment of briefing when I took my stroll. No one had said, *Stay a minute*, when I had risen to announce I would stretch my legs, no one had said, *We need you to go over this with us*. Neil and Mole might have begun planning whatever this was yesterday, or the day before, or on a session that Neil spent on Mole's platform.

"What site?" I asked.

"Nearby," Mole replied. "You'll see."

It would have only emphasized my position on the outside to ask, *What site?* again. Mole was driving Cathy's car, and Neil automatically took the seat up front beside him. Every time, in fact, that we had been given a ride anywhere, Neil had taken the front seat, except when the four of us had been driving down from the woods and Mole took the front beside Cathy. It seemed there was

an invisible but clear marker of agency on each of us so that hierarchies could be assembled in a moment, and Neil obviously out-
ranked me.

Or maybe it was based more on sexuality than power. Maybe
Neil subconsciously took the empty front seat so that Mole and I
wouldn't be paired together. An interesting thought, one that made
me see Mole, his weather-creased eyes, his mix of sinewy toughness
and surprising delicacy, in a new light. Already, seeing him with
Cathy had shaken any category I'd been tempted to put him in. He
was very smart, without having had much apparent education. In
fact, the role he seemed to play most was that of patient teacher.

Mole drove the Beltline that skimmed through greater Eugene
and the more recent housing developments verging on outlying
industrial yards. He exited and turned past a lumberyard, the
clean-edged wood in varying board thicknesses stacked neatly on
pallets, forklifts zipping here and there. Down the road a bit was
a square white stucco office building whose signage declared it to
be WAINWRIGHT TIMBER CORPORATION. Mole pulled into the lot,
parking in a space facing the entrance.

"We need someone to go in," Mole said.

"Why?" I asked.

"Possible action site." He turned to address me. "You look the
best out of all of us. You game?"

By "best" I grasped that he meant "straightest." I was wearing
clean khaki shorts and a white tank top, sandals that were not
meant for the woods.

"Go in and do what?" I asked. Wouldn't there be security cameras
trained on the entrance, tracking my every movement, digitalizing
my face?

"I want you to draw the ground-floor layout when you come out," Mole said. "You're good at drawing, right? How about just asking the receptionist for a job application? Tell her you're a college student looking for summer office work."

"What do you mean, 'action site'? What are you going to do?"

"I don't even know, maybe nothing. This is all preliminary."

"But what do you need a floor plan for?" I pressed.

"Think of it as scouting. Out in the forest we monkey-wrench the machines, maybe some midnight we'll come and do the same to the files in the office. Same goal: Fuck up the operation."

"You mean arson?"

Mole screwed his whole body around toward the back, his expression a mixture of amusement and exasperation. "Darlin' Emerald, I don't know *what* I mean. Haven't you figured out yet that we make this up as we go along? We scout, we wait and see."

I looked at the kindly creases around his eyes, the way his smile came from his eyes instead of his mouth, hidden between the mustache and beard. I liked Mole; I believed in his judgment.

"Does Mudman know about this?"

"That's not how we operate," Mole explained patiently. "We work in small cells, all pursuing common objectives, plans unknown to each other."

"They'll see my face."

"That won't matter. You won't be connected. I need somebody besides me to go in and look around. And River here"—sideways tilt toward Neil—"doesn't look like a convincing office temp."

Neil turned back to face me. He tried to reach for my shoulder or arm, his fingertips just brushing me.

"Whatever you want to do," he said. "No one's forcing you."

If I said no, what point would there be in staying any longer? I could be privy to no one's plans, trusted with no job. Neil would move further into the work and I'd be finished with it. Wouldn't that be the same as splitting up?

No one had prepared me for this. Or had I not been listening? Had I not wanted to hear?

This was simply a walk inside to request a job application, look around, jot down the floor plan when I came out. I wouldn't be connected to any monkey-wrenching, if it even occurred. Didn't I want a clean job? Didn't I agree with the movement's objectives? I'd seen the clearcut. I'd become intimate with one of the largest and oldest trees left standing. I did want to save it from the obscenity-calling men with their ripping saws.

"No pressure," Mole said. "But we shouldn't sit here too long in the parking lot if no one's going in."

"I'll go in," Neil offered.

"No, I'll do it," I said. "It's just that you sprang it on me."

Mole smiled apologetically. "Sorry. Secretive by habit, I guess."

I crossed the parking lot self-consciously, trying to scan for cameras and seeing none, though they might be tiny, perched like birds in corners and shadows.

The receptionist was a pleasant auburn-haired woman in her forties with reading glasses on a chain. She held down a small island in the middle of a lobby that offered carpeted halls leading left, right, and behind her.

"Help you?"

I made a plausible applicant. She willingly coughed up a form and foraged further for a clipboard and a pen. Would I like to take a seat and fill it out here?

The straight-backed chairs were vinyl and chrome. I fished in my bag for my agenda book, ostensibly to look up addresses, but really to slip a small piece of paper onto my clipboard. It took only a minute to sketch a rough floor plan.

I finished by jotting some fake information on my form to look industrious. As I worked, a tall silver-haired man in jeans and a spruce-colored denim shirt, carrying a nylon briefcase, came striding down the hall chatting with a more dressed-up but obviously subordinate colleague stretching his own gait to keep in step. The tall man had an air of being in charge—an easy smile coupled with the businesslike steeliness of his spectacle rims and eyes behind them, the body language of being alpha, turning only the side of his mouth toward the other as he talked, while the second man torqued his whole upper torso toward the taller man so as to hear every word. They paused upon reaching the receptionist, the taller man reaching automatically for a wad of pink message slips while it was the other man's turn to talk. I heard only bits, something about harvest units at Devil's Rake, a pending sale I recognized from campfire talk, some volume and acreage numbers. The receptionist, who seemed to have a sympathetic flow of energy with her boss, caught the direction of his gaze and supplied the sotto voce explanation that I was applying for summer office work. A few minutes earlier, I had folded my small map and stowed it in my back pocket.

"Sounds good, Gary," he said, clapping his hand on the subordinate's shoulder. "Call me with those figures when you get them."

The big guy gave me a friendly smile, and I saw that he was in the habit of being kind to his secretarial staff. The receptionist leaned a couple of degrees in his direction as if a compass needle sensitive to magnetic north, and I, too, felt a slight flaring of my pulse, an impulse to pay attention. I almost forgot who I was pretending to be, a Ms. Andrea Brooke, of a random house number on Cathy's street, a University of Oregon student on summer break, and irrationally hoped to find favor with him.

"How are you?" he said.

I told him I was fine, my adrenaline firing. An easy man to like, I thought. A fair boss. Probably a good father, judging by the way he seemed ready to take an interest in me. Not a man-woman interest, which plenty of other fifty-something men wouldn't hesitate to communicate in their smile, but a fatherly one. I don't know how I knew this, having no father of my own, but I did know it. Nothing hungry there.

"We have anything at the moment, Verna?" he asked over his shoulder.

"Maybe some hourly word processing and filing," Verna replied. "Marcia's going on maternity leave, and there are vacations coming up."

"You a student at the U?"

I nodded, truly terrified now, already making adjustments to my story, my data. I was trying to remember Cathy's profile so I'd have some plausible information to offer him.

"You ever run into my son, Josh Wainwright? Business major. Senior."

I pretended to think it over, then shook my head.

"Of course not," he said, a small chuckle at his own naïveté. "Big place, the U. Well, see if Paul's around to talk to her, Verna."

He left the building flipping through his messages, already pulling his cell phone out of his pocket and pushing buttons.

Verna obeyed, speaking into her phone to see if Paul was first in one place, then another.

It hadn't occurred to me that I could be offered work. I don't think it had occurred to Mole, either, or we would have cooked up a more complicated alias for me. Now I saw that my hastily scribbled lie sheet would get me into immediate trouble. I could refuse to talk to Paul; I could invent some reason to leave, tell Verna I'd come another time. Or I could ask Verna for a fresh application, tell her I wanted to print a neater version (impress her with my perfectionism), put my actual name down: a transfer student from the East, looking forward to her first term at the U. Nothing I'd said had contradicted that. I could wow Mole and Neil. I could walk out of Wainwright Timber with an inside job as myself. I could find ways to be a true mole, xeroxing documents, making more elaborate floor plans, listening in on conversations. I had about two seconds to decide as Verna punched numbers, seeking Paul.

I'm not sure why I recopied that application. I know I was confused by liking the place, the secretary's kind face, the warmth of Mr. Wainwright in the few seconds he spared to chat with me. I didn't stop, just then, to analyze how his air of authority, subtle affluence, fatherly nature registered in my comfort zone. The lobby was hung with enlarged black-and-white prints like the ones I'd bought as postcards: loggers from the turn of the century whose expressionless faces were somehow sexy in their refusal to acknowledge the behemoth trees they sat astride or leaned against. Sexy, too, the dangling suspenders, the grimy open collars, all that evidence of work and fatigue. Mr. Wainwright owned this place, that tradition. The other prints that hung behind Verna were lush color prints of the Cascade forests, one with a dagger of sun slicing down through the green, as you'd perhaps find yourself impaled by a ray of light slipping through the clerestory at Chartres. My senses, my instincts and cravings were confused. I could work in this pleasant place; at the same time, I could help the movement. I wasn't in a position, in those few minutes of jotting my correct name and Social Security number (I'd have to, of course they'd check it), to sort out the inconsistencies.

The interview went well. Paul was the personnel director; perhaps he had hired the men who had come out to the forest and called us cocksuckers and assholes and threatened to cut us down. He didn't seem awful, just conventionally ingratiating, and not too bright, or he'd have probed for reasons why I'd leave Wellesley one year short of a degree and transfer to a state university in the West. Changing majors, I'd said. Now fully committed to studying Northwest anthropology. Fortunately, he didn't care to get to the bottom of this and moved on to my word-processing speed. He tested me, found me proficient (I'd been keyboarding since fourth grade), conferred with the office manager by phone and offered me hourly employment starting the following week. In my state of excited uncertainty, I accepted.

I found Mole and Neil the way I'd left them, elbows out the open windows of Cathy's car, listening to a Chieftains concert on tape. Neil raised his eyebrows and reached a hand out to touch me as I approached.

"You were gone a long time," he said.

I liked the wavelength of their expectancy as I got in the back, not minding that it was the back now as they twisted around to see me, as I stretched out and occupied the full warmth of the vinyl bench seat.

"Let's get going," I said. "No offense, but I don't want to be seen in your company, guys."

"Well?" Mole demanded as he drove carefully and conservatively away from Wainwright Timber. I suddenly wondered how I was going to get out there every day; what I would use for clothes; if, in fact, I was going to show up on Monday.

"What took so long?" Neil asked. "I was about to come in and look for you."

He was, too. I had never seen him so protective, still stroking my arm as he reached back for it.

"It takes a while to apply for a job," I said. "First there's the form, then there's the interview, then there's the typing test."

Mole hooted, his eyes finding mine in the rearview mirror. "You actually went through with all that?" he asked, his voice merry.

"The question is," I continued, "do I take the job?"

Neil's face was a mix of surprise and concern. "They hired you? You didn't give them your real information?"

I felt a wave of misgiving.

"I wasn't going to, but when it looked like someone was going to talk to me then and there, I had to have a way to make it more legitimate." I explained the blend of truth and fiction I'd used. How I thought maybe it would be good for the movement to have someone on the inside, as long as I couldn't be connected to known activists.

Mole was drumming his fingers on the steering wheel as he drove. He looked back at me again, his face respectful. "You're right," he said. "Let's think it through, how best to use this." I was fully a member in his circle, or his "cell," now. *My* name was on the application, *my* lies.

"I don't like it," Neil said.

"I need to think about it more myself," I countered. "When I went in, it was with the idea that I could always pull out, that I was merely preserving an opportunity."

"Absolutely," Mole said. "What we've got here is an opportunity. A potentially huge opportunity. Great job, Em."

I tried calling my mother when we got back to Cathy's house. Neil and Mole were hanging out in the backyard drinking a beer, Cathy was away at class. The bedroom was dim and cool and smelled slightly of Neil's and my sweat, and I lay on my back for a few minutes before pressing the digits of her cell phone number. I had her on speed dial, but I needed to go slower than that. Too fast, too fast, the dissonant tones of the automatic dialing. She would swoop up her cell phone on the second or third ring, and there would be her large bright self, too insistent and too eager. She had a warm, sandy voice, the kind that would play well on National Public Radio, a voice meant for making people say more than they intended. I hadn't heard it in almost two weeks, and now the thought of it enveloping me, trying to penetrate my mood and discern meanings she imagined behind my meanings, made my heart suddenly rise up against my rib cage like a flustered bird.

Then the fourth ring, and the fifth, and I knew I was safe, that I could satisfy whatever urge I'd had to connect with a message about being in Eugene and that everything was fine.

The first syllable of her answering message fooled me for an instant, as it always did, its slightly out-of-breath quality making me think that she had picked up after all. But no, it was the recorded Ginnie, confident and confiding, a citrusy note of irony in her voice as she said, "It's Ginnie's voice mail. Leave a message."

So I did, trying my best to give her something, anything that would help, our two voices passing remotely, without the dangerous spark of actual contact jumping between our accumulated tinder.

13

When I was in high school and my mother sometimes worried I wasn't working up to my true potential, she'd scare me with the bogeyman of secretarial work, as in: "Fine, don't do the extra credit problems, don't stretch yourself; a high school degree is all you need to be a secretary." In my mind clerical work had come to represent everything oppressed and degraded and self-sabotaging about the female condition. Not that she perpetrated these regressive hierarchies herself: she and Preston made their own coffee in the office, went out of their way to hire male clerical help as well as female, and never asked employees to do anything vile like pick up dry-cleaning. My mother's fear of trammeling fellow women in a gender-determined occupational bind was so sharp that she actively encouraged her best female secretaries to leave her, suggesting law school at night, or at the very least paralegal training. Sometimes she'd produce a shame in them so acute that they'd quit in confusion, finding less emotionally taxing typing and filing elsewhere.

For the last two years, their secretary had been a round-shouldered, wheezing Luddite named Maryanne, swollen of ankle and heavy of sigh. When Preston asked Maryanne to organize a file or type up a bill, she'd comply silently and relatively efficiently. When my mother presented her with work, however, she communicated through a raised eyebrow or a pursed lip that she'd been disturbed in the midst of certain other pressing tasks.

"It's because you sound like you're apologizing, Mother, every time you give her something," I'd told her last summer.

"I'm certainly not apologizing for anything, Julie. I've run a law office for almost thirty years, believe it or not. I don't think I need you to tell me how to speak to my secretary."

"I'll bet Preston would be glad to fire her for you if you just say the word."

"No one is firing Maryanne. Enough!"

But something about Maryanne cowed my mother, whether it was the way she'd push herself up from her desk and make a show of pausing for breath, or the fact of the two buses she had to take to get to work, or possibly that she'd never married and the specter of a bleak old age filled with penurious circumstance and lonely ill health was plain to see, looming over her shoulder.

It was Maryanne who'd proclaimed any technological upgrades to the office computer network unnecessary, thus rendering half the attachments that got e-mailed to the firm impossible to open because Prince Baylor was still chugging along on some near-beta software while the rest of the world was zipping by on version X and beyond. It was Maryanne who invariably "forgot" to change toner cartridges and left them for my mother to do, requiring her to take off the jacket of a good suit and stain her hands before court. It was Maryanne who'd perfected a range of hostile and sullen greetings for the public when they phoned.

"Aren't you afraid she'll drive away business?" I'd asked. I loathed Maryanne, missed the affable Lisa, who had quit to be more available for driving her three children to their many after-school engagements.

"Julie, what *is* it with you?" my mother demanded. "Can't you leave poor Maryanne alone?"

"You see!" I'd said. "Poor Maryanne! You *need* her to be pathetic and incompetent, don't you? Why would it undermine you to have good help?"

It was the last time we discussed it, and I'd sensed for a while that I wasn't welcome in the office, at least on my mother's side of the suite.

Maybe she subconsciously intended that Maryanne be an object lesson for me so I'd never lose sight of my Prince responsibilities. My grandfather, a stooped, balding man who, when he was alive, had always been kindly with me but never less than formal, had been in the habit of making little speeches about contributions the Prince family had made to society. I could feel him revving up for one of these talks when he'd make a slight throat-clearing noise and look not at me, but through me, as if seeing one of my more gifted ancestors in place of the disappointingly formless child at his table. He had drilled all the venerable ghosts into my memory: the clergyman who'd founded societies of good works, the crafter of legislation ensuring better conditions for laborers, the string of abolitionists and suffragists of both sexes.

Grandfather himself had sat on the bench of the state Supreme Judicial Court for three decades, a position that left him with the habit of seeming to weigh each word spoken to him for truthfulness. It was understood that I'd take my position, as my mother had, among the admirable cast of thinkers and doers, as soon as my inconvenient period of childhood was behind me.

The irony for me was that now here I was, officially grown up (or at least I would be in a week), inhabiting a public cause with my whole self, though I'm sure Grandfather Prince, if he could have known about it, would have been just as disapproving of the mission and its means as my mother.

I hadn't called her in a week, ever since I'd become a summer clerical worker for Wainwright Timber. I didn't have the heart to tell her I was proving to be an excellent secretary, filing swiftly and without error, having the kind of fully developed conscience that required I leave no folder in irregular order, even if I'd discovered it in an alphabetical or chronological shambles. Everyone seemed to love me: the other office workers, Verna, Marcia, and Amy, because I made their lives easier and was no competition, being only temporary; the managers because I took on typing projects with cheerfulness; and Mr. Wainwright himself, who never failed to stop when he saw me to exchange a word about the U. Fortunately, his interest centered on the sports teams and the business school, about which I could claim utter ignorance. The more I told him (true) things like I'd never once watched a college basketball or football game, even back in Massachusetts, the more it tickled him. He took to calling me "the intellectual," but with such good humor I didn't mind.

Mole was delighted with the xeroxes I presented him with—

land surveys and environmental studies, internal memos about which timber sales would take priority, correspondence with the USFS and other agencies.

"This stuff is terrific," he said as he leafed through each new batch. "Mudman is beside himself—no one ever thought of putting someone right inside Wainwright. It's brilliant."

It is smarter to read the documents rather than burn them, isn't it, Mole? I wanted to chide, but didn't, because I took such pleasure in his praise.

Neil fretted that I was too exposed. "It's too risky," he'd said to Mole on several occasions. His worry excited me; it seemed to demonstrate that whatever his commitment to the ideas we were fighting for, his commitment to me was just as strong. "If any of this stuff makes it on the website it's going to get traced straight back to her."

"We're not going to use any of this in a way that will lead to Emerald," Mole argued. "We can act on what we find out without implicating her in the least."

"What if she gets caught making the copies?" Neil asked.

"No one scrutinizes my work," I told him. "I'm one of them; we've done our female bonding." I held out my recently manicured fingernails as proof, but I felt bad making fun of them. Marcia, who was going out on maternity leave next week for her first baby, had suggested the manicures and pedicures on a recent lunch hour.

"I can't reach my feet anymore," she'd said. "Besides, when my feet are up on those stirrups I don't want to be staring at chipped polish, you know what I mean?"

The thing was, I hadn't been acting when I leaned back in the chair sighing with pleasure as my heels were pumiced. Where I came from, serious women didn't do nail polish. So it was a guilty pleasure to return to the self-adornment of high school and junior high, to spend a long minute weighing the wisdom of Barely Pearl over Sandstone, before finally deciding on the silvery pink tones of Cockleshell.

Marcia had almost gone for a rerun of Racing Red, but something in her pending maternal status must have caused her to revise her judgment at the last minute and jump over to Deep Rose. Those decisions made, we'd leaned back in our padded vinyl chairs and had given ourselves over to the sensual heaven of being groomed.

"Your legs are so perfect," she exclaimed as the attendants massaged us toes to calves with lotion. She sighed. "Enjoy it. I never used to have these before, either." She pointed to the purple network of broken capillaries outside the bend of her knee.

It was the first time I felt disloyal then, not to Wainwright Timber—which as a corporate entity was, I now concretely understood, wholly profit-driven—but to Marcia, whose cotton shorts were hiked up in the chair at an unflattering angle that exposed the marbled slab of cellulite on the underside of her thigh in addition to her inky web of spider veins. I murmured something about them being too faint to see and closed my eyes so I wouldn't have to. Pregnancy didn't look to me so much like glorious blooming as it did a state of siege, one's body puffing with fluids and internal pressure until the woman inside looked like she was going to bloat right out of her skin. I didn't see how Marcia could stand coming to work every day, needing to rotate her wrists and ankles in circles every half hour to keep the water from pooling into fat little sausages at her extremities, but she told me that the distraction of being busy and having the AC was way better than refolding the layette for the umpteenth time in a hot house. She was teaching me how to write purchase orders and keep inventory of the office supplies. It was easy work, but she marveled at how quickly I caught on to everything, and I almost regretted that I wouldn't be working as promised through the entire summer so I could make sure that she came back to a perfectly organized desk and PO log.

I wasn't sure how long I would stay, but I wasn't counting the days or anything until I could quit. My mother always preached the virtues of having work you could "own," but now I saw the advantages in having work you only inhabited for the few hours you were there. It was almost a vacation from the self; there was a peculiar satisfaction in how finite and immediate your goals were, and how necessary to others you could make yourself.

At work I was almost beginning to believe my cover, think of myself as belonging to the U of O and not Wellesley, as being genuinely interested in the anthropology I claimed to major in, even to the point of buying a book on the history of the Klamath Indians that I read on my lunch hour. Or tried to read, since usually one of the other women would plunk herself down beside me at one of the picnic tables out back. The patio had probably been part of the original plans for the office building, but the amenities I'm sure came from Mr. Wainwright himself. There was a gas grill, on which he barbequed hamburgers and hot dogs himself on summer Fridays at noon for the staff. A badminton net was staked into the expanse of grass beyond the cement, and though I had yet to see anyone actually play, the fact of its presence seemed to encourage us to think of ourselves as free beings who could pause in our employment when we chose to strike up a game.

Despite this, and his uniform of blue jeans and work shirts, no one worked harder than Mr. Wainwright. I had the feeling he and my grandfather would have had a great deal to say to each other over dinner at the Harvard Club had they chanced to occupy the same plane of time and space. Grandfather would have approved of the younger man's treatment of employees, and Mr. Wainwright would have been admiring of my family's work ethic. They would have silently noted each other's lack of showiness and plain manner of dressing (I automatically put Mr. Wainwright in a tweed blazer and U of O striped tie for the occasion, and he dressed up just fine—just as I had seen him turned out once as he hurried from the building for what must have been one of his meetings with legislators). They would have cut into their steaks—medium rare—with appreciative attention, skipping dessert and topping the meal off with whiskey. Mr. Wainwright was about the right age to have been my grandfather's son, the one he never had. Baseball did not seem to be his sport, as it had been Grandfather's, but I'm sure he would have been a genuinely interested audience for Grandfather's reprise of the Red Sox's tortured history, post-1918.

So used was I to thinking of Mr. Wainwright in these benevolent terms that I experienced a double shock one afternoon when I was coming from the xerox room with a stack of files and a set of copies I'd just made—the complete correspondence between Mr. Wainwright and a pro-timber Republican state rep about harvest methods around the Slap Creek watershed. In the instant of seeing him swinging around the corner, covering several feet per stride in his unhurried gait, the man in the letters—"*our mitigation measures will substantially reduce stream input, turbidity, and temperature elevation, and cause no alteration in channel morphology in the watershed area, as per guidelines in the Replacement Volume program*"—and the man coming closer in the corridor, smiling as he saw me, fused into one. How impossible that they be the same person! The first terror was the certainty that I was about to be caught; the second was that it would be by Mr. Wainwright, who would be disappointed in me.

If he stopped to see what I was carrying, there would be no explaining it—no one had requested to have these files pulled. Wainwright had obtained the rights to these units last year, and cutting could begin as soon as the USFS obtained a Biological Opinion from the National Marine Fisheries Service on the status of the salmon that ran through some of these streams. Mr. Wainwright was a salmon fisherman himself; he'd once pointed out a varnished specimen that he'd had mounted and hung in his office on an occasion when Verna had sent me in with some letters for him to sign.

"Chinook," he'd said. "King of salmon. That one there's three feet long. You ever eaten any?"

I'm sure I had, out to dinner with my mother. I'm sure some waiter, somewhere, had extolled its virtues—line-caught, swimming in the Columbia the day before, flash-frozen and flown to Boston on ice for our dining pleasure that night. I shook my head, because he seemed to require that it be unknown to me, that he be the one to introduce me to its exquisiteness.

"Stick around," he said. "We'll try to get one on the grill for our Labor Day picnic. Nothing like it, basted in a little butter and lemon over an alder fire."

As he grew nearer in the corridor, my mouth was probably agape like the shellacked trophy on his wall, because he trimmed his smile with a slight look of concern.

"They're not working you too hard, are they?" he said.

I affirmed they were not, gripping my files.

"Good girl," he said, and was past me.

I wondered what would have happened to me if my cover was blown—would I simply be fired, or worse? At that moment, I couldn't think of anything worse than being exposed before Mr. Wainwright.

In all, I was weirdly pleased with my borrowed life, cooking dinner with Mole and Cathy in her tiny kitchen while Neil surfed the web or checked e-mail; making sweaty love to Neil in the spare bedroom (Cathy's roommate was in Guatemala for the summer, and I'd told Cathy we'd sublet the room for July); rising early to go with Cathy to her yoga class at the U before showering and using her car to go to work. One afternoon, when we were picnicking in Baker Park after I came home from Wainwright, I asked Neil what he and Mole did with themselves all day, fearing that he was growing bored and thinking of going back to the woods without me.

"We're making plans, checking some things out," he said.

I gave him an exasperated look.

"Do you really want to know?" he asked. "Think about it. You can guess the kind of stuff, can't you?"

I could. I'd been glancing through *Green Riot* at the Vine, and while I didn't think Neil was as radical as the fringe group that

planned to blow everything up, I knew he was avowedly indiffer-
ent to legalities, maybe even impatient for his moment to step
definitively into a fugitive life. Some of the memos I'd xeroxed for
Mole showed that repair bills for sabotage the elves had done
came to thousands of dollars. More important, the continual barrage of interference was genuinely handicapping. The Wainwright
managers were furiously lobbying any and every law enforcement
agency they could for greater surveillance, and on some projects
they had tripled their own security budget.

"I'll tell you if you make me," Neil said, taking a bite of his
sandwich, "but I don't want to. You're already risking enough."

The deeper we got into the movement, the closer we'd
become. Neil had been passionate all along, but now he couldn't
resist touching me more often, wherever we were, as if he were
making sure I was still there. Lately he seemed slightly off balance, less sure of himself, making unfunny jokes about me aban-
doning him in a month for—here he'd clench his jaw in a
pseudo-Brahmin accent that I'd never actually heard anybody at
home use—my *muh-thah in the Back Bay.*

But the defensiveness was flimsy, and I knew he was tense.
Sometimes in his sleep he mumbled, or he would wake with a
start and reach for me as though an uncomfortable dream were
clearing behind him and he needed my help to keep ahead of it. I
knew all this had to do somehow with the work.

"You're not going to get hurt, are you?" I asked. I suppose I was
conceding that I didn't want to know the specifics.

He laughed a little and said, "I won't if you won't."

I wondered if the laugh meant that he was disappointed, that I
should have probed and faced whatever he and Mole were doing

with their days while I was busy making sure that bills of lading were filed in correct order. I opened my mouth to say something, then closed it.

"What?" he said, taking a swig of his water and lying back down on the blanket. I was sitting up, cross-legged, eating salad out of the Tupperware we'd borrowed from Cathy's kitchen. He ran his hand along my bare leg, then up under my short denim skirt, his finger tracing a light line across the crotch of my panties.

"Stop," I said, "you're making me spill my salad."

He pulled his hand back.

"Are you still writing that thing for *Green Riot*?"

He nodded, crossing his arms behind him and lying back.

"How come not for the *Register-Guard*, or some other press with a wider circulation? Isn't writing in *Green Riot* kind of like preaching to the converted?"

He shook his head. "They'd edit too much. *Green Riot* will print what I write whole, and it's important to me to create a complete record. I'm considering a series of essays over a year or two, kind of a *Walden* of the forest movement."

A year or two. I ate a couple bites of salad in silence.

"And that's it for academia?" I asked. "For the dissertation?"

His finger was back, running up and down along my thigh. He was studying me now, staring. "God, you're beautiful," he said. "You're so, so beautiful."

"Don't change the subject. You always change the subject when I talk about your dissertation. I don't mean that you *should* go back to academia, it's clear that you feel much freer outside it, it's just . . ." I paused, hating how much I sounded like my mother.

"I mean, you've completely ruled out using your degree in some agency?"

Neil laughed and removed his hand from my leg. "What degree?"

He was being purposefully thick, just to annoy me. "The degree you just got. The doctorate. It could be worth so much in the right place. You could help make changes, make policy. Be *constructive.*"

I was afraid he'd accuse me of being Ginnie, or tell me we'd already been through all this, but instead he just lay back on the blanket.

"There isn't any degree."

Why couldn't he just talk this through? Why was he being so perverse?

"What are you talking about?"

"There's no degree unless I rewrite a crucial aspect of my thesis to satisfy Rick fucking Driscoll. That's what I'm talking about."

I was lost. What did his advisor have to do with it? We'd celebrated the thesis, the defense, the honors, the degree.

"You didn't finish?"

"Oh, I finished. Just not to the satisfaction of *Dr.* Driscoll." He said the title "Dr." with such acid that I knew he would never be one.

"But—if it was just a rewrite he wanted, I mean, what *did* he want?"

"It's not important now," Neil said, closing his eyes as if a great weariness pressed upon them.

"It's important to me. To understand."

Neil took his time, maybe gathering his strength. Then he sat up to face me. "I used economic algorithms to calculate the value of old-growth acreage based on multiple worth factors including habitat preservation, scarcity, scenic importance, and recreational use. Quantifiable variables. I performed the circus routine per-fectly. But the whole project sickened me. So I put my feelings—unpardonable academic sin—into the argument: I asked, why submit the sacred, the mysterious, the ineffable to a test of proofs? Why speak the language of money when the whole point is that it shouldn't have to be about money?" Neil searched my face. "I refused to revise. Take out 'the ineffable,' and all that. So, no degree."

"Why did you lie about it? Do you think I would have cared?"

"Don't you?"

"No. I mean, I care that you were screwed over, and I care that you didn't trust me enough to tell me about it, but otherwise"—I shook my head—"no."

He reached up and took my salad from my hands and put it down on the grass beside the blanket and took hold of my two hands and pulled me toward him so that I had to rise up slightly on my knees, uncrossing my legs behind me and coming to rest against him. He undid the chopstick thing that was securing my loose topknot—the day had been unbelievably humid—so that my hair fell around us like a curtain, providing a kind of privacy as we kissed, his fingers finding their way back under my skirt.

"Not here," I said, freeing myself, moving back out of his reach.

He groaned and lay back in the grass, letting me go. I watched him for a few seconds, his clenched face.

"You're so funny," I said, tracing his cheek with a finger. He'd been crazed lately, so thirsty, so needing to be held. My finger came to rest on the artery on the side of his neck. I held it there, felt his pulse leaping against it.

"Don't tell me that. You think I don't know? I'm a fucking freak and always have been. You said it yourself—the *different drummer* nerd, that's me in a nutshell," he mocked.

I was taken aback. "No, no," I said. "I didn't mean—"

"I love you. This freak *loves you,* okay?" He said it fiercely, as if we'd been arguing. He'd never said it before, though I had, the second week of knowing him. I remembered offering it impulsively, shyly, then flushing hot from the shame of hearing no response.

Now it was my turn to be speechless. I wanted to say—was forming the words to say—*I love you, too,* but he'd caught me so off guard that somehow I couldn't summon them until they began to seem awkwardly late, out of sync with the moment.

Thunder rumbled in the distance, and a fat drop or two splattered on my arms and Neil's forehead. He didn't seem to notice.

"It's going to storm," I said, springing to my feet and pulling him up to a sitting position. The air was charged with a sulfurous light, the green of the park edged with its yellowy aura. It was incredibly sharp and beautiful, I could suddenly hardly bear how beautiful.

Then the rain began hammering down and I said, "*Hurry,*" though I don't know why—I welcomed the rain. In this famously wet state we'd only had a few showers since we'd been here. I began gathering up the picnic containers and then tried pulling the blanket out from under him but he was just sitting there, watching me with a little smile on his face.

"You're being a dope," I told him, laughing. Finally he let me drag him to his feet and toward the curb where the car was parked, but then he stopped and shook me off. He stood in place to open his mouth to the sky as if drinking, offering his throat to the thunder and the heavy drenching rain as if it were the alpha dog and he was the young pup and he meant to show it that he meant no harm, that he recognized its greater power.

He yelped, he barked, he howled at the rain. I stood back and let him be. I watched him howl.

Then he came and wrapped his wet self around me, kissing me, nipping me lightly with his teeth, howling, telling me again that he loved me, and this time I felt no need to try to answer, there was nothing to say because it was all about him filling up the whole world with this sudden wild energy. He didn't stop when a car drove by the sidewalk, spraying our legs with grit, and he didn't stop when another, a few seconds later, honked at us. I let him hold me, wondering what would come after this outpouring, this flood.

I drove home, peering forward at the road through the ineffective swipes of the wipers, rubbing circles against the windshield with my hand because Cathy's defroster didn't work well. We didn't talk and went into the house, which was empty and felt like it belonged to us, and he followed me into the roommate-in-Guatemala's room, except we had claimed it now, with our smells, with our fluids and our sweat. He stood still and watched as I peeled the wet clothes away from myself, and then let me set to work on his, until we were both goose-pimpled flesh, damp and chilled from the rain though the house was humid and warm. We stood embracing, and he was taking his time now, we had all the time we needed. We were in an undiscovered country he had taken us to with his words and he seemed new to this—an appre-

ciative tourist—ready to go slowly and see everything, feel everything. His hair smelled like him and like the rain; his cock nosed
against me. But still we just held on and swayed slightly in the
silence we owned, until we were so rich with it that he could dis-
card the silence and say it out loud again, this language of the
new place he had taken us to.

Then I said it back to him, as I was ready to, finally, just in his
ear, though the sound of it might have gotten lost in our breathing together as he cased me onto the bed and pushed inside me,
my silvery pink fingernails splayed against his back, my voice
slipping away in the tide of my own thoughts, in rhythm now,
trying to find the place I knew something from, just out of reach,
the idea of it, still coiled—he was, we were, just reaching it
together now, just touching the empty heart of the matter, of a
scrap of time pulsing silvery pink, and I had it now so I could let it
go and let it come at the same time, because the heart of it was
quite contrary, the heart of it was nothing, everything, rhyming,
chiming together, like *silver bells, cockle shells, pretty maids all in a row*.

14

never actually decided to ride along the night Neil and Mole
planted the bomb at Benito Ford under the row of black and silver Explorers. By which I mean, yes, I was in the car, entirely of
my own free will, and yes, I knew the mission, which was to send
a dramatic, news-at-seven type of message to the SUV-owning,
gas-guzzling, environmentally thoughtless American consumer.

But it was not a decision made in the sense of weighing my
position and committing to a new course of action, a revised philosophy. Nothing so deliberate. I was not even completely clear
on when or why Neil's focus had shifted from the forests to these
other, infinitely numerous causes, though his argument in the
essay he was writing for *Green Riot* was that there was no separat-
ing one aspect of environmental preservation from another. It was
pointless to save the forests while destroying the ozone, or to
save a particular species from extinction if the eroding global

habitat threatened all. I did see the logic of that. But his thinking had also evolved in other ways, having to do with methods and means. When we first arrived in the forests, our forms of resistance had involved peaceful occupation of the cutting zone, and—though Neil and I had not directly participated in it—sabotage of the logging equipment. I think we all viewed such sabotage as defensive, destroying that which was bent on destroying the trees. As his scope widened beyond the forests, so did his notion of what kinds of acts constituted defense.

But I knew that Neil wanted to let things live, and that was how he differed from the darker voices in *Green Riot* that were so disaffected they could only destroy. Because I believed this about him, and because I could see the ultimate truth of his positions—and, I guess, needed to test my own—I was in the car that night.

There was also this business about us, so unfinished and confusing. Lately Neil had been asking me to stay with him beyond the summer, into the indefinite future. I wouldn't remain at Wainwright, of course; already I'd gathered as much information there as I could as a clerical temp, so I'd given my notice. I'm not even sure what good my petty espionage had done for the movement, but at least I'd felt useful during the last month. The more I'd read the company memos that were so self-justifying, so tilted toward profit and market, the more I'd felt aligned with the cause of conservation, sure of my role and my contribution. Without my little underground job that so played to my strengths, I'd have to find something new to do. Neil wouldn't have cared, I suppose, if I'd just started lying around reading novels—but if we were to keep what we had, this shared purpose, this *heat*, I'd want to be part of the work.

I had so far refused to discuss August because I didn't know what to say. There was something about his newly explicit affection that left me a bit flummoxed. I'd grown used to the Neil who'd kept everything inside; from the start I'd needed to read in what I meant to him, what we meant to each other. I thought I knew. I'd concluded that he loved me in his fashion, up to his capabilities, and that it just wasn't in him to belong to a person as much as to his ideals. Without consciously deciding to, I'd been coming to view him as someone from my past, someone who'd opened my eyes to important things and undone complacencies I'd had and who'd been my First Important Love. I hadn't stopped loving him, but I couldn't see myself staying satisfied in the role of the accommodating woman behind the great man—and I had no doubt that he would become a great man after his own fashion. If, as I thought, his work would always come first, if he had no need of another person in a deep, abiding way—that just wouldn't be enough for me.

Now, though. The emotion coming from him was all the more overwhelming for having always been held in check. A force, a claim on me that was almost frightening. It seemed his capabilities were not stunted after all: he could love in a large way. The discovery had me more than a little stunned.

I wasn't sure why my impulse was to hang back, considering. Wasn't that taking the overly analytical, overly detached position I'd judged as evidence of his own shortcomings? But I was still processing the change, and if I didn't quite trust what he was so suddenly holding out, then only time would test it.

But that didn't help, since it took me to the August question. I hadn't called my mother in weeks, since the message I left after being hired at Wainwright. She'd called me, of course, many times. At first I'd merely turned off the ringer, letting the phone vibrate or flash when her calls came in. More than once I'd be startled by the phone's urgent awakening in my pocket, the creepy way it felt alive as its vibrations buzzed into my hip. At night, to keep the buzz from rattling the nightstand table, I'd change the answer feature to flash, and I'd be jerked out of a doze by its sudden, lighting eye. Finally, to keep my sanity, I'd turned the phone completely off and left it in my backpack. Once a day I'd power it up and scroll through the newest barrage of her recent calls, checking to see if any were from Preston. If Preston had called, it would mean something was wrong at home.

But they were all her phone calls, and though I knew she knew I wasn't answering, I still refused to hear her ring or call her back. What, after all, could I tell her except lies? The truth was in my silence; that I was somewhere far from her, and that she'd have to let me be there without her for the time being. If we talked, she would start telling me what to think or do. And, in my confusion, I simply *could not stand* to hear her voice right now.

Even that day, my twenty-first birthday, I didn't call to speak to her, though I called the home machine at a time when I knew (prayed) she'd be at the office to say: "I love you, I miss you, I'm safe but might be out of touch a while longer. Eat cake with Preston and relax about me, okay? Be glad I'm not one of those sorority chicks who gets shit-faced and spends her twenty-first birthday projectile vomiting. Such is the ethos of my present company that I'll probably drink nothing stronger than a little organic hard cider. Bye, Ma. Kiss, kiss, hug, hug."

After leaving the message I felt cleansed of guilt but orphaned, if temporarily and intentionally. I didn't know why I hadn't told Neil my birthday was coming up. I'd kept meaning to, then I'd forget it myself, for days at a time, until the thought would pop up, *I'm going to be twenty-one.* I knew there'd be no big dinner out, nothing wrapped, nothing like that. It was pretty clear Neil didn't operate that way. Maybe I'd kept the whole thing to myself to forestall any disappointment, the awkwardness of having Cathy feel she should put together a special dinner, the flatness of having Neil simply wish me a happy birthday.

Neil didn't know it was my birthday, though my friends at Wainwright knew. I'd planned my last day of work to coincide with my birthday, and though I'd been in their midst only a month they had a supermarket cake for me at lunch, decorated with a little tipi to signify my anthropological endeavors, inscribed with green and yellow icing to note my status as a University of Oregon coed: HAPPY 21ST AND GOOD LUCK, JULIE.

Tears actually came to my eyes when I saw it, which made Verna start dabbing at her own behind her glasses. Paul darted in for the corner piece of cake with the most icing, and even Mr. Wainwright ambled through, declining cake but leaving me with a little cardboard folio containing a Borders gift card addressed "to Wainwright's guest intellectual." He gave my shoulder a pat and said, "If you ever get tired of that library stuff, we can always find you something to do around here," and then left us to answer his ringing cell phone.

When Marcia dropped in for a surprise visit with her days-old son, Matthew, his red face and pugnacious expression in startling contrast to the placid yellow ducks on his onesie (the outfit I'd given her at our lunchtime shower), I went beyond feeling misty to needing a Kleenex to blow my nose.

"Oh my God, Marcia, he's great," I said, after I'd honked my way clear enough for speech. He began squalling then, such a funny, fierce-looking baby. Though he was her first, Marcia had somehow acquired this absolute maternal assurance; I marveled that she knew exactly what to do to quiet him in an instant. Then, so generous, she handed him over to me, even before Verna and the others, and because he decided to accept this, acknowledging the change by merely gazing at me searchingly, I started feeling the hot pressure build behind my eyes again. These people were so *nice*. What did they know about me? I mean, even if what they thought they knew about me was true, which it wasn't, what did they know even then? Nothing, yet they were ready to believe only good things, ready to make me part of their celebrations and cakes, ready to wish me the very best. The fact of their kindness coupled with my deceit, the impossibility of ever being real to them, was what made me want to cry, and I was not a crying person.

"He's so big," I said, jiggling him a little, just in case he was getting ready to wail again. Matthew stared in a distracted way at my forehead, as if there were something fascinating printed there.

She rolled her eyes. "Tell me about it. Nine pounds, five ounces. Twenty-three hours of labor."

"Ouch!" Paul offered from his place by the coffeepot, depositing his paper plate into the wastebasket, indicating this conversational turn was where he'd take his cue for exit.

"You're damn right, ouch," Marcia called after him, which seemed to quicken his pace. She laughed. "Dave used to be like that. You should hear him now, going on like some kind of obstetrical expert—how many centimeters I was before the epidural, how many pushes it took, what a great job he did cutting the cord . . ."

I had a vision of Neil bending over me in concern, in amazement. Wouldn't he? Or would he never allow himself that, the most purely hopeful kind of act—making a child?

Verna leaned forward to offer her finger to the baby and I felt obliged to hand him over, though I swear he kept staring at me, swiveling his head to keep me owlishly in view.

"He likes you," Marcia said. "How about some babysitting when you're a student again?"

"Oh, absolutely," I lied, though I wanted to half believe at the same time. Maybe I would still be here; maybe I would stay with Neil, and the roommate in Guatemala would never come back and I'd find something to do in Eugene that interested me, whether it was the trees or art or—who knew? Maybe the anthropology of the Northwest Indians, retroactively make an honest woman of myself.

"You look great," I said, secretly taken aback at how pregnant Marcia still looked, but I was glad I said it because she immediately looked so grateful.

"You're lying, but thanks. I'm trying. Fifty sit-ups twice a day."

My Cockleshell polish from our joint manicures was chipping away and I'd yet to buy any remover to take it all the way off. I was reluctant to lose it all at once. It was better to see it get ugly and strange-looking first so I wouldn't miss it when it was gone.

Before Marcia left I scribbled down her number, telling her that mine was only temporary (almost the first true thing I'd said) so I'd call her instead to set up a babysitting date. When I didn't call she'd assume I'd gotten sucked into my studies or my social life and she wouldn't think any worse of me for that. She'd check to see if Verna had a new phone number for me, and when Verna didn't, I'd gradually cease to exist for either of them.

Verna insisted that I leave early. It was true that I'd gotten everything so caught up, in my zeal to leave things perfect, that there was nothing really for me to do. I promised to drop by soon to say hello, and then before I knew it I was on the walkway I'd slunk up a month earlier. For a moment I was almost confused myself as to what my actual business at Wainwright had been. As I said my goodbyes it felt natural to suppress the knowledge of all my deceptions and think of my weeks there as merely a summer job. I had the final paycheck in my pocket to prove it, and I intended to buy myself some kind of birthday present with it, I didn't know what.

Mr. Wainwright left the building a minute after I did, after I was already out of sight behind the wheel of Cathy's car. I was glad we hadn't run into each other one last time. During my whole employment I'd liked him, had found myself trying to make a good impression not because it would solidify my cover but because I wanted to, bizarrely repressing that I was there to undermine his business in any way I could. I know it didn't make sense. I couldn't help thinking of him as a good person, and for some reason I was able to do this, split Mr. Wainwright and Wainwright Timber into two separate entities, one which I admired on the basis of nothing much more than the way he talked about his son and treated his employees, the other which I was battling as a greedy and destructive corporate interest.

I had three hours to myself in the afternoon, and I used them to wander a bit downtown, having tea at the Unicorn, a more feminine hangout than the Vine. Cockleshell nails were okay here. Women and womyn of all persuasions were welcome, and I loved to slip away and have tea and read in one of its many little rooms, each distinctive in its Victoriana. My favorite nook was no bigger than a broom closet—it probably had been a broom closet, though now it was decorated with a wallpaper of nettles and birds. I sat at a minuscule table with a lace cloth that reminded me of a fortune-teller's shawl, reading in the weak light that filtered down from the high window facing the alley. It was a room only big enough for two—one person in each wicker chair across the glass-topped table—and though I enjoyed my privacy, I also yearned to have a long, meandering conversation with a friend.

I thought about calling Frida from here. She would love this secret, cloistered spot. But in order to make sense or say anything real, I'd have to catch her up on too much, and the things I wanted to tell her couldn't be shouted over a cell phone. The intimacy of the little room would be wasted, since she couldn't share it with me, and anyway, I'd probably catch her in the middle of her workday, interning at a big ad agency. I'd called her once from the road, and she could only talk for a few minutes but said she was having a terrible time, the tasks they gave her were petty and demeaning, and she was cynical about the whole enterprise and jealous of my freedom and "real work" as an activist. I told her to quit, then, and she'd said maybe she would, but there was something energized and even happy in her voice that told me she was exaggerating her boredom and probably, on balance, enjoying it well enough. Frida could be a bit of a drama queen about the bourgeois expectations her parents had for her, but she always ended up succeeding beautifully at each stage and seeming quite pleased with herself.

At home I would have spent this evening bar-hopping with her, or maybe being surprised by something else she'd rigged up with friends. My mother would have taken me to dinner wherever I wanted to go, and she would have racked her brains to come up with the perfect present, something lasting like a lithograph or a first edition; Ginnie was good at stuff like that.

I finished my tea, resolving to go home and find Neil, tell him and anyone else who was around to come out and help me celebrate. This was the birthday I could claim to be an adult, so it wouldn't be very mature of me to spend it moping around, irrationally hoping that someone would divine my secret.

He and Mole were at the kitchen table drinking a beer.

"Hey." Neil reached out to draw me to him. "You're early."

"Well, you know, last day," I said. "And it's my birthday. They sent me home."

Neil's eyebrows shot up and he cocked his head back to look up at me. "Your birthday?" he sounded taken aback, even hurt, and it occurred to me that I might have completely misjudged him, that not telling him had been insulting.

"Twenty-one." I had to offer it all up now, not just any birthday but *the* birthday. This was what I had withheld.

"You're just telling me now?" He pulled me onto his lap and looked across at Mole. "She's just telling me now."

"Happy birthday," Mole said. He rose, put his bottle in the recycling bin, looking embarrassed. "Want a beer?"

"I guess I should, huh?"

Mole got me one from the refrigerator, twisted it open and handed it to me.

"Cheers."

I accepted it and lifted it in silent toast. I felt like a fool.

Mole made some excuse and left us, and I slipped from Neil's lap to take the seat he had vacated.

"I didn't want to make it a big deal," I offered. He was still staring at me, his expression unreadable.

"It's kind of a big deal," he said, "don't you think? Twenty-one?" Then he shook his head. "Wow. I keep forgetting how young you are."

"Fuck you," I said, trying to keep a bantering tone, though I thought he had no business patronizing me. "Maybe I keep forgetting how ancient you are."

"It's true. All those wasted years jumping through hoops." He said this disgustedly.

"Don't say that. You haven't wasted anything." I tried to turn the conversation, ashamed of my earlier lack of faith in him. "Let's celebrate or something. Let's get a party together. Or," I groped, not sure how to make things right, "let's go out to dinner, just the two of us." I thought he understood by now that I could pay. I didn't want to make things worse by offering.

"Yeah, sure." He rubbed his jaw, clean-shaven again after I'd convinced him to get rid of the stubble he'd acquired during the tree-sit. "I just wish I could have known the date ahead of time, that's all. Mole and I had something planned."

"Oh, well, if you've made *plans*," I said.

He didn't bother to look exasperated at my tone. "An action. But it'll work out. We'll celebrate your birthday first. We don't need to prepare until late. The action will be very late. Maybe you'll want to ride along. Let me check with Mole."

"Check with him? You need his permission to bring me? After everything I've done at Wainwright?" I really was angry now, thinking all at once of things like my automatic place in the back seat when the three of us rode together, of all the conversations and planning that happened outside my presence. "Am I one of you or not?"

"Well, I guess that's something you have to decide," Neil said matter-of-factly. "No one's keeping you out of anything."

"All right," I countered, holding his gaze. "What's the action?"

Neil paused a beat, and I saw how the secrecy had already become ingrained, how it meant I would always feel like I was prying things from him.

"We're going to mess up a few SUVs on a car lot."

I was the first to look away. It was true, I supposed, no one had been keeping me out of anything, except me. Did I have the stomach for the kinds of things he was up to now? I'd come across the downloads on explosives, the little snips of copper wiring left on the kitchen table when I'd returned from work. Could I be part of that? Maybe if I went along tonight, if what he was doing took on an actual shape and scene that I not only witnessed but was part of, I'd have to decide how I felt about it. "Let's go back to the trees," I'd said to him in bed one night, when in the dark his tossing had kept me from sleeping. "Isn't that what we came here to do? Isn't that what we're suited for?"

"Yeah," he'd said. "I want to. But first I need to take things further, follow the implications of believing in radical change, radical acts of self-defense. I can't write about it if I leave the dangerous work to everyone else. Don't you see? It would be fraudulent. I'd be nothing better than a parasite."

I'd tried to see, and in a sense, I did see. *As long as no one gets hurt;* that was my line. He'd assured me it was his, too. But when we said it was okay to move from jammimg up logging equipment to exploding things, how could you guarantee anything? Didn't the line itself then fracture into shrapnel, dangerously jagged and random?

He'd continued to lie awake for long parts of the nights, keeping me awake, too, though I'd finally slip away from him into exhausted sleep, dreaming turbulent things I didn't remember in the morning.

I hung on to my image of the real Neil heading back to the trees to write, perhaps me with him writing something of my own, the two of us figuring out "the implications of our beliefs" together, as well as what it meant to belong to another person. Sometimes a year away from Wellesley didn't seem long at all. There was always the chance that after a year I'd fail to see the point of ever returning. Perhaps I'd arrive at a place where I wanted nothing to do with the value system implied by a Wellesley degree, would willingly jettison its privileges and associations in a way I hadn't quite been able to do yet. Neil had turned his back on all that, had achieved what seemed a state of complete liberation where he was guided by his own set of moral imperatives rather than "society's tut-tuts." Was it really in me to do the same?

We all went out, Mole, Cathy, Neil and I, for burritos and a pitcher of beer. I remembered my message to my mother, and vowed not to be the twenty-one-year-old barfing on the floor in the bathroom. But it was my

birthday, and these were my friends, and I stopped trying
to count the glasses as they were topped off, a jumble of foam-
ing fractions I'd try to add together and lose track of. Around
ten a band started playing, and Mole pulled Cathy onto the
dance floor. Neil just sat there, apparently unmoved by the
music, and I told myself, *So okay, he doesn't dance, lots of guys don't*,
trying not to feel disappointed in him, in myself, for sitting out
what was a very good band on my birthday. We watched the
others, Neil drumming his fingers from time to time on the
table, not because he was carried along by the rhythm but
because of his impatient inability to see the point of it, glancing every now and then at my wrist since he didn't wear his
own watch. *Be here*, I silently admonished him. *Be here now with me.
This is important, too.*

The music turned bluesy, and Mole took Cathy's hand, leading
her in a very creditable grinding swing, making it even less likely
that Neil would volunteer to dance, since evidently there was a
bit of skill involved. When the next song exhibited a more standard rock beat, I thought to hell with it, and touched his arm, saying let's go.

He hung back, a grimace of distaste or maybe embarrassment
on his face, but I just stood there looking down at him until he
shuffled to his feet. He danced in an arrhythmic, but not totally
spastic loping style, sort of primate-like, but it didn't matter to me
what he looked like, the main thing was that I was dancing on my
birthday. It was the second time that day I'd rescued myself from
self-pity by simply figuring out what I needed and doing something about it, and so my good mood started to come back again,
even better than before.

We danced until we were sweaty and Cathy and I were lifting our hair off our necks and using napkins to dry our faces. Earlier, Neil had tossed his flannel shirt on the table; his T-shirt was now damp from his heat and redolent of him, of our sex. It looked like he'd been enjoying himself. *See?* I wanted to ask. *Sometimes can't it just be about pleasure? Be simple?*

Mole and Neil got in line to order another pitcher and I watched Cathy polish her wire-rimmed glasses and slip them back on. I liked her, had gone to yoga with her half a dozen times, performing downward-facing dog and low cobra in her company. I had accepted her hospitality and cooked side by side with her in her cramped kitchen. I had borrowed her car and even a couple of things to wear for work. But did I know her? Not a bit. She was blond and cool and too serious to be really attractive, though she could be pretty when something melted in her face and she laughed outright. I thought of her as the "mathematician," though she claimed that she had no idea what she wanted to do after graduate school. Neil was the only one she could really explain her thesis to, and I could see something similar in them, the way the universe appeared to them in a pattern of logic and inevitability, a way they had of approaching something new as if it weren't so much to be wondered at and appreciated as it was to be quantified and solved.

Mole's easygoing confidence seemed to loosen Cathy's tightly organized nature. She even moved more easily when he was near her, as if his own physical assurance carried over. I wondered how much her involvement with the movement was simply to please him.

"Did you know they're going out tonight on an action?" I asked her.

"Not really. I mean, I pick things up, but I try not to."

"Don't you approve?"

"I don't know what they're doing, so I don't approve or disapprove." She said this primly, establishing her boundaries, her glasses glinting at me.

"It is complicated."

She let this go unremarked.

"I might go along," I said, wondering as I watched Neil and Mole moving back through the crowd if I meant it.

"I wouldn't," she said sharply. "But if you do, make sure you don't talk about it, all right?"

Maybe it was then I decided to go with them—as an experiment, yes, but also to establish my difference from Cathy, from her timidity and smallness. Clearly her safety meant everything to her, whereas for Neil the issue was always: What's right? What's required?

When they got back to the table I saw why it had taken two of them to go to the bar. They had come back not only with the pitcher but a piece of key lime pie ornamented by a single wooden match planted upright in the middle.

"No candles," Neil explained.

"But they gave us two matches, so we're set," Mole said, clearly satisfied with their ingenuity.

I'd saved the candle shaped like a 21 from my office party cake. It was in the bottom of my bag, wiped clean and wrapped in a paper towel, but I didn't mention it now.

"This is great," I said.

Neil scraped the spare match on the side of his boot and lit the one standing in the pie as candle. It hissed into a flare, then burned steadily, the wood withering under it. I had to blow while they were still in the middle of singing to me, before the pie could smother the flame.

When I opened my eyes, they were still on the last line of the song.

"Did you wish?" Neil asked.

"Yes," I said, pulling out the little blackened stump. It left my index finger and thumb sooty. Though I hadn't exactly wished; my desires were too inchoate to separate into simple wishes. The best I had been able to manage was, *I'd like everything to be all right.*

"Don't tell," Cathy said, for the second time.

15

"Has it ever occurred to you guys," I said from the back seat, "that we're riding in a car this very minute? I mean, that's obvious to everyone, right?"

I was a little drunk. Maybe more than a little. But not shit-faced. We'd returned to the house, where Neil and Mole had disappeared into the tumbledown garage for an hour or so, nothing much out there but boxes of damp books belonging to Cathy and her roommate. The fact of them out there rigging up their project under the bare bulb hanging from a rafter had made me want to giggle, it seemed so Hardy Boys, so Wile E. Coyoteish. Even tipsy, I knew that giggling was inappropriate, especially when I looked at Cathy's blank face, the way she refused eye contact and wished me good night and shut her bedroom door with a non-negotiable click. I imagined her having her evening green tea and writing in a journal, documenting her whereabouts: *Twelve seventeen a.m. Said good night to all. Saw no one until morning.*

I leaned forward between the two front seats, an elbow perched on each one, unwilling to be excluded.

"It's an irony, isn't it?" said Mole, who chose to take me seriously.

"It really, really is." I had a feeling that if we just kicked this around a little, we could get to the bottom of it. I was feeling mathematical myself right now, as if life's equations were out of whack and we needed to do some erasing and refiguring to get them to line up.

"Consistency's important, right? I mean, here we are, going to blow up a car dealership—that sounds so dramatic, doesn't it?—and we're riding in a car."

"That's true," Mole agreed, considering this.

Neil was quiet, though he reached back and put his hand on my wrist. It was the only part of me he could reach without contorting himself, but I somehow didn't like that it was my wrist. I felt his tension, and because I wasn't tense but strangely exhilarated, even giddy, it seemed childish and unreasonable of him to be tense. Wasn't this whole idea his? Didn't he think it was a good one? Then why be tense?

"Look. One thing," I said.

Mole met my eyes in the rearview mirror.

"Let's not do anything like this to the Wainwright building." I twisted my wrist free of Neil's grip. "The people there are really nice. Verna? She's the receptionist? She came in today—or I guess it was yesterday now—with this cake for me because it was my birthday and my last day. And Marcia brought her new baby in, he was amazing."

No one answered from the front seat. Mole was looking at the empty road ahead, the parking lots of the mini-malls deserted. We were in a strange car that Mole had left in Cathy's car to go borrow. It had unfamiliar smells and wrappers. Who in the movement would eat at Burger King? How did Mole come up with a different car every time he needed one?

"Promise," I said.

"You know we can't promise that, Em," Mole said, looking in the mirror again. "You wanna talk about the bad guys, they're it."

I thought of the Borders card from Mr. Wainwright in my bag, the way he'd told Marcia to leave early whenever she needed to during her last month. He was holding her job open for her.

"You're the one that gave us all their memos," Mole continued. "The one about commissioning their own study to show that spotted owls were adapting to second-growth forests? The bullshit report they cooked up on timber salvage and burn management?"

I didn't want to talk about the memos; I knew all about them, and was behind whatever constructive use the movement could make of them. I only wanted to let them know how kind Verna was, how adorable Marcia's baby.

"But you never do anything in the middle of the day," I said. "Never ever with people on the scene."

"Of course not. Look at us now."

Look at us. All the more visible because it was two-thirty in the morning and we were the only car on the road. If we drove past a cop he'd make a mental note of our plate and make, just in case.

Neil straightened in his seat and I guessed that we'd arrived, a sprawling Ford dealership with a sea of glossy SUVs and pickups.

Mole drove past the entrance to the rear of a darkened convenience store.

"This is where you can pick us up in fifteen minutes," he told me. "You've got your cell phone turned on?"

I nodded.

"We'll call you if there's a change in plan. Otherwise, drive around on some main streets and circle back here."

They got out to remove a black nylon duffel bag from the trunk and I hopped out, too, suddenly halfway to sober from a surge of adrenaline, unready for this to actually happen.

"Mole, whose car am I driving? In case I get stopped. What do I say?"

"You're driving your friend Jimmy's car," Mole said smoothly. "Coming home from his house. Make something up. You're good at lying."

I opened my mouth to protest this, and then shut it. Was I?

Neil gave me a dry kiss, and I tried to make it more significant, more of a message between us, but he pulled back.

"You'll be fine," he said, patting my arm.

"You will, too. Right? Be careful."

We all froze as a siren wailed by a street over, a squad car rushing somewhere having nothing to do with us.

"One less to bother us," Mole said. "Let's go."

I watched them walk around the chain-link fence that separated the convenience store from the lot and disappear into the shadows between the angled new cars. The night was fresh for July, crisp dry air that felt more like September, and I wanted to remain sitting in place with my windows open, watching the time slip by on my lit cell phone face. It seemed important to focus on those numbered minutes, that in my slightly dizzy state if I looked away I'd lose my bearings and screw up the plan. Shouldn't I just stay where I was? I'd be lots more conspicuous driving around, so nervous that I would probably do something stupid and get pulled over. And hadn't I had way too much to drink to be behind a wheel? Why hadn't that occurred to any of us? Whoever's car this was—and I hoped to God it wasn't stolen— did they really want me getting it impounded?

I opened the glove box to see if there was a registration and found that this six-year-old Honda Civic belonged to one James McMillan of Grove Road, Eugene. My friend Jimmy's house. I couldn't pull that off, I *wasn't* good at lying. When I'd interviewed at Wainwright, and later worked there every day, I hadn't been lying, but acting. I'd been inhabiting a role, one that could almost have been true, and sometimes felt like it was.

I decided to stay put. Two minutes had already melted away. What were thirteen more? What would I say if a squad car pulled up behind me right now, its spotlight sweeping the interior of James McMillan's car, illuminating the Whopper sandwich wrapper on the floor? I'd say I was rummaging for change, stopping to get a newspaper from that box. I peered out the window; did the box even have any papers left? It didn't look like it. God. Stay or go. At least if I was moving, it would look like I had a reason for being on the road. But sitting here? What would I say? That's why Mole had wanted me to drive. He had thought all this out and I shouldn't second-guess him now. But the drinking part. He hadn't factored in my panic, my blood alcohol level. In fact, my whole presence was a last-minute alteration, getting to ride along some sort of a birthday present, the way a cat presents you with a mangled mouse or a dead bird, its neck neatly snapped.

Stay or go. Three minutes gone. Twelve to wait, hyperventilating in the dark, or eleven to drive, arms trembling at the wheel. The light of my phone kept going off, programmed to save my battery, and I kept hitting the button to keep it lit, needing its steady company.

Maybe I should pull the car forward slightly, a little more deeply in the shadows in back of the store? But Mole had parked here. Who knows what he and Neil already knew about the ideal placement of the car, the existence of motion-sensitive lights in back of the store, or even a security camera? They'd spent days and days on their secret activities, making plans, scouting things. If Mole parked the car here, it was for a reason. I would not move it, unless to drive away, which was what he'd told me to do in the first place.

Four minutes gone. Mole and Neil might be done more quickly than they figured, might come back in nine or even eight minutes, instead of eleven. That would be a reason for staying put. I wouldn't let myself imagine the opposite, that they could be delayed or somehow hurt—what would I do then?—that eleven minutes could stretch into fifteen. I couldn't stand being back at fifteen; starting over from fifteen was unthinkable.

The pressure building up in me was beginning to feel dangerous. I didn't think my heart had ever been so jammed against my breastbone, not during cross-country meets when I'd set school records, not when I'd waited offstage to make my entrance in *Brigadoon*. It was like something breaking in my chest, a force beyond tempering.

Five minutes was a third of the time. Too late to go now.

But I needed some air, more than the window could let in. I opened the car door slightly, horrified by the noise it made, the squeak of James McMillan's front driver's door. If a cop found me crouched outside the car, I could legitimately say I was sick, that I needed some air. That I'd had a little too much to drink and had decided against driving farther. I'd tell him I was about to call a cab.

That would win a cop's sympathy! He'd be delighted with my good judgment, moved to help out in some way. He might be a father, like Mr. Wainwright, all the more interested in seeing me keep out of trouble.

It seemed like a brilliant solution at the time, that I had solved my problem completely. I didn't stop to think that the whole thing would backfire as soon as there was an explosion to investigate, a police stop to document someone's presence in the vicinity.

That reasoning didn't intrude. I welcomed my release from the hell of my indecision as I practically tumbled out of the car and sat on the ground by its side, letting the breezes sting my forehead where the sweat had beaded. I thought of the message my mother had left me for my birthday, and I almost punched my code to hear it play again, hear her voice now, but thought better of it in case Mole needed to reach me. I knew what it said:

Jules, happy birthday, sweetheart. You have no idea what it meant to hear your voice, to hear your jokes. Please stay safe. Please check in again—I'm calling from the cottage, so you can reach me there or on the cell. I hope you have a memorable, joyful day. I'm expecting that I'll be seeing you sometime next month, can't wait. We'll have a belated celebration then. Then, after a slight pause, *Say hi to Neil.*

It might have been the first time since meeting him that she'd uttered his name. He'd been "your friend," spoken in such chilly tones that there was no mistaking her hostility. It was as if, at that single meeting, she'd seen directly into Neil and his contempt for everything she stood for, everything Grandfather had stood for. Had she also seen forward to this moment, her daughter crouched and sweating in the dark at two-thirty—no, two-thirty-seven now—in the morning? Seen how far he could go beyond common decency, how far he would take me with him? I hadn't been swept along. She'd be underestimating me if she thought that. Neil was no Svengali; though he'd pointed the way, I'd paused at each juncture, considering if I could follow. And sometimes I'd pointed the way. I had thought of going inside Wainwright. I owned that particular contribution.

Say hi to Neil—the saying of his name, the admission that he was real; a major, major concession. The only birthday gift she could give from the distance she was at, and I had some notion of what it must have cost her.

Two-thirty-eight, not my birthday any longer, and several hours past it in my mother's time zone. It struck me that she had dawn now, maybe a dawn she was sitting up to watch with her hands warm around a coffee mug, the sky pinking up beyond the scrim of our kitchen curtains. We both liked the kitchen best of all the cottage rooms, its homely oak table and windows on two exposures, eyelet curtains lifting in the salt breezes that were carried from beyond the afternoon insect hum outside the screens. When we were at the cottage my mother spent inordinate amounts of time there where her mother had puttered before her (in those days with a "girl" to help), and outfitted, as Ginnie liked to point out to visitors, with the same forties gas range and stalwart Frigidaire that somehow chugged on.

Continuity, she liked to say, deliriously cheerful over the way everything stayed the same at the cottage, no beginnings or ends. A daughter at the table reading a library book, a mother crimping a pie crust made from ingredients listed in the handwritten book of *Family Recipes,* Grandmother Rose's version calling for lard which my mother dutifully shopped for in Edgartown. The only break with the past was the smooth black loaf of the microwave that chirped periodically to announce my mother's reheatings, for she would only take a sip or two of her coffee before forgetting it again, absorbed back into the process of rolling, crimping, blanching the heavy peaches that our neighbor invited us to pick, slipping the round fruits free of their skins with a quick thrust of the paring knife, the glistening halves spiked with fibrous red tentacles around the pits like miniature solar flares. There she was, my mother, offering me a slice, and there I was, shaking my head—*Why not?* Because I was reading, and showing her I was not to be disturbed. Or maybe, simply because she was offering.

I had a sudden longing to go back to Boston, back to Wellesley, back to Frida and my mother and an ordinary life. If this was what Neil was really going to choose, this darkness, this life underground, then he wouldn't, in any real way, be making room for us. And no matter how righteous the movement's ideas, this, now—this shivering on asphalt beside dumpsters at two-thirty in the morning, thinking up stories to tell cops—felt debased, beneath any of us.

*   *   *

jumped at the crunch of gravel behind me, my heart leaping up again. But it was Mole and Neil, their faces blank.

No one spoke, and I didn't know if things had gone badly or if they were simply as terrified as I was. I dove in the back seat and Mole and Neil took their places in the front, the duffel at Neil's feet. Mole started the car and since he was behind the wheel it was a reassuring sound, not the earsplitting roar it would have been had I started it up alone.

I sat back limply, exhausted, watching the ordinary sights slide by, the closed gas stations, the Dunkin Donuts, the Borders where I could spend my gift when I liked.

"Well?" I asked.

"According to plan," Mole said. "No one noticed you?"

He didn't ask whether I had driven or stayed put, and I chose not to bring it up.

"No."

"That's fine, then. I think we did it."

Mole dropped us at the house and went to return the car from wherever it came from. Neil and I slipped into the unlocked front door and went to lie down in our bed without undressing.

"What time will it go off?" I asked, after we were twined together.

He raised his head to look at the clock on the nightstand. "Not yet."

"When?"

"Four-thirty or so."

It was almost three-thirty. I didn't feel like I could possibly sleep until the bomb exploded, though I wouldn't hear anything from five miles away. I know they must have thought about everything, checked before for a night watchman. Mole had said, had promised, no people. Thinking about metal ripping apart, images of fire and flying debris, my heart started thudding again, keeping time with the seconds as the red minutes melted from one number to the next. I tried to concentrate on the moment of transformation, when the straight lines that formed one number blinked into a new figure, and always missed it. Neil was silent beside me and I knew he was not asleep.

Somehow I did sleep, sometime before the numbers lined up to be four-thirty. I kept jerking awake seconds before impact in continuous dreams of falling. I'd spend a few drowsy seconds wondering how the brain could do that, so convincingly simulate a fall that I could have *sworn* I had just landed with a thud, although softly, safely, because remarkably, it was a bed that I had fallen to. Then I'd drift back and do the whole thing over again, like playing at death, and getting to live every time.

16

I awoke around dawn and rose to look out the window, half expecting to find a world of ash. Everything looked the same: the small weedy lot that was our lawn—Cathy's lawn, not mine—the neighbor's gray-weathered leaning fence, the mint-green duplex across the street. I saw no one, though soon a few people would be out to walk dogs, go for early morning runs. It was Saturday, so most would sleep in, have a leisurely breakfast when they woke up. Mole had a wickedly good recipe for berry pancakes, and the marionberries had been ripe for a week now; Cathy had bought some at the co-op yesterday.

How much of an accomplice had I been, squatting by the side of the car, holding myself across my stomach? What was the damage now?

Neil had finally fallen asleep, only just. I knew that he had been awake most of the night because every time I woke ahead of

one of my jerked landings, he was there to catch me, saying, *Shhh,
it's all right,* and petting me back to sleep. Now it was his turn.

When we slept in the trees, I woke this early every day, but
rarely otherwise. When I did, it felt as though I had given myself
the gift of an extra day within the day—time seemed infinitely
generous when you were awake at sunrise. You could see vistas,
you could let an intention gradually take shape.

My first inclination was to do some stretching, then walk,
shake away the cramped fear of last night. After that, I would
make pancakes for my roommates. The clarity of my desire last
night to go home was already being dimmed by the thought of
missing them. I turned to watch Neil sleeping for a minute, his
mouth slack, his brow smooth. He looked so young. He was
seven years older than I was, more educated, I'm sure smarter, but
I felt, looking at him, as if I were the one who needed to protect
him. I thought he had no idea what he'd begun. My dream
deaths, so harmlessly drilled in my sleep again and again, redemp-
tion offered every time by waking, had made me feel how sweetly
improbable real rescue was. Only a roll of the dice had caused
some police cruiser to turn one way instead of another. It was
mere chance that I'd woken in a bed this morning with my
boyfriend to feel the sunrise, expansive and free in front of me.

I came in from my walk to find Mole already up, sitting in
shorts and a T-shirt at the table with coffee. His hair was standing
up in all directions, his eyes still rimmed with sleep. A glorious
breeze came through the open window, lifting the limp yellow
curtains.

"So," I said, pouring myself a cup of coffee. "You look like shit."
He ignored me.

"Good morning to you, too," I said. "I thought I'd make your famous pancakes. That all right? Do we still have those berries Cathy bought?" I turned to rummage in the refrigerator.

"The timer didn't go off," he said.

I straightened to look at him. "What do you mean? How do you know?" My first thought was relief; we hadn't done damage.

"I did a drive-by just now. I had to see."

"Well," I said, at a loss as to what to say, "I guess it was a wasted night."

"Don't you see? It got stuck or something. But anything could jar it into motion again. It *will* go off."

"When?" I asked, though it wasn't a real question. Asking *when* was only a small wedge placed between what he was telling me and the incipient horror I was beginning to feel.

There had been a BONUS BUCKS DAYS banner in the showroom window, bunches of blue and white balloons tied to the cars, CASH BACK placards in the windshields. Saturday was a big day on car lots, and this Saturday the air had an agreeable snap to it— a preview of back-to-school air, and wouldn't the moms in particular feel a buzz from that, a need for change, sprucing up, something nice and new to pull up to the curb in for drop-off?

"You have to stop it, Mole," I said.

He stared at me with that look that seemed unfocused, so unlike Mole with his crinkled, laughing eyes.

"How?"

"You have to make a call or something. Before they open."

He shook his head.

"Why *not?*"

"Sacrifice ourselves?"

"Mole, *families* shop for SUVs. Families with *kids.*"

"I can't help them."

"Mole, come on! Remember in the Vine you were arguing with N—River—about the middle class, how they could be marshaled to the cause with their contributions and signatures on petitions—"

"Not these people. These people are making a choice."

"How do you know *who* they are, Mole? You're not God. What if they're there to buy the *little* car"—I groped for a make—"the fucking Fiesta or something?" Even as I was trying to argue with him in his own terms I heard the absurdity of it—that some people might be worthier of life than others based on their MPG ratings.

"Mole, this is sick. When you were a logger, you didn't want any deaths on your hands, remember? Now that you're an activist, it doesn't matter? *Mole?*"

He didn't answer. It was eight o'clock. I didn't know how early they might open on Bonus Bucks Days.

"I'm going to wake up Neil, you don't have any right to decide for him."

"Stop saying his name. For his sake."

Cathy came into the kitchen wearing a kimono and looking apprehensive at the tone of our voices. "What's going on?" she asked.

"Nothing," Mole said.

"There's going to be some talk about last night, Cathy," I said. "If you don't want to hear it, you should go for a walk or something."

She gaped at me, and then looked at Mole, who refused to look back at her.

"Are you in trouble?" she asked him.

"No. If Emerald will let it rest."

"There's no resting right now, Mole," I said, my voice rising. "You promised there would be no people."

"I never promised."

"You did!"

"I said we worked at night to avoid people. Which is what we did."

"Someone got hurt?" Cathy said, looking from one of us to another.

"Not yet," I said. "Not if Mole makes a call."

"I don't want to hear this," Cathy said, putting her hands over her ears like a child.

"Then don't listen," I said. "Mole. I'm waking up River. I'm going to ask him if he wants to get with me in the car—"

"Not my car," Cathy interrupted.

"—go with me to a pay phone and make a call. Is *that* all right with you?" I didn't wait for an answer. I went to the bedroom and found Neil sleeping just as I had left him, a thread of spittle on his cheek.

I shook him, speaking low and urgently, trying to explain through his groggy state how the timer hadn't worked.

"Whaa?" he said, propping himself up on an elbow.

"The bomb, Neil. It's going to go off with people around."

He sat up all the way. "It wasn't supposed to do that."

"But it's going to. And Mole's not going to do anything. I'm making a call from a pay phone. Do you want to come?" I didn't need him to come, but I wanted confirmation that he would choose to make the call. If he, like Mole, would not, I needed to know that.

"If Mole says—"

"Fuck what Mole says. Mole's willing to blow people up. Are you?"

He looked up at the ceiling as if the answer might be written there. The clock said eight-ten and I was not going to wait for him to search his soul.

"I'm going now." I turned to leave, and heard the bedsprings squeak behind me as he swung his feet down to the floor.

I thought, then, that I had not been wrong about him. Whatever he was willing to do in his "radical defense" of the planet did not include harming people. I had not been wrong to love him.

We left the house without speaking to Mole or Cathy. I'd put sneakers on for my early morning walk, and now we ran, like two lovers out for a morning jog, toward the university.

We found a public phone along a walkway. People were strolling or jogging past, not looking twice at us.

Neil told me to go beyond and wait for him under a tree.

"Both of us," I insisted. Did I want to remain to verify that the call was made? I didn't think of that then. I just wanted to see it through.

It took less than five seconds to report a bomb at the Benito Ford on the Beltline. I saw him dial, I heard him speak.

After he hung up, I looked around to make sure no one was around and wiped the receiver with a balled-up napkin I had in my pocket. I smiled at him and shrugged.

We held hands and strolled with the others through campus. On Thirteenth Avenue we found a café and ordered lattes and croissants. I realized I was starving, and ripped into mine before I could even pause to spread the strawberry jam I had asked for. The croissant was buttery and rich and I ate it in about five bites.

I ordered another. I was hungry, hungry, hungry, and the melting pastry on my tongue felt like reprieve, like forgiveness. We had done this terrible thing together, and we had undone it, or I hoped we had. It was ours. How could I leave him now?

Finally I could slow down, some of the voraciousness gone, and lean back, drinking my coffee in warm sips rather than gulps. Whatever adrenaline had propelled me out of the house and to the phone booth was ebbing, leaving me shaky instead.

"I can't believe what almost happened," I finally said. And then, because he didn't reply, just stared out of the window at the people passing by on bikes and in running gear, I pressed, "Can you?"

He shrugged, then said in a low tone, "It was unfortunate. And I'm glad we made the call. But that kind of thing's always a risk when you—"

The waitress appeared, looking pointedly at me and my two plates and two latte cups, asking if we needed anything else.

"We're fine," I said.

Neil waited until she had tucked the ticket by a saucer and left us. Then he continued, "It's a risk, that's all. You've got to be realistic about it."

"Realistic!"

He gave me a warning look. I leaned forward and said softly, "You're quite calm about it now, Neil. But I've been sleeping with you for the past month, and I can tell you that your sleep isn't calm. Your dreams aren't calm. You're in denial if you think you can pretend this is no big deal."

He glanced at the check, then reached in his pocket and laid out bills for the whole thing, a gesture so swift and uncharacteristic that I was momentarily distracted by how unfamiliar it was.

Then he stood, and I had to almost scramble to my feet to keep up with him.

When we were outside, he drew close to my face and said savagely, "It's a big deal, Em, okay? It's a fucking huge deal. You wanted to be in it, you're in it. This is no time to get sloppy by running off at the mouth in public." Then he steered me by the elbow around some sidewalk tables until we were by ourselves on an empty stretch of tree-lined sidewalk and I jerked my arm free of his grip.

"It's Julie," I said, fierce tears springing to my eyes. "My name is Julie."

He shook his head, whether to deny me this or to show his impatience, I couldn't tell.

"And don't tell me what to do!" I said, raising my voice.

He shrugged. "No problem," he said, quickening his pace so he was a step or two ahead of me.

"And don't act like you're so in control, like you have it all figured out!" I was practically screaming now, as he pulled even farther ahead.

Then I stood still and did scream, to his departing back, "You have *nothing* figured out, *nothing*!"

He waved a hand vaguely behind him, a dismissal, as he turned the corner onto Cathy's street.

I was furious that I was crying, that he refused to stay and fight, that I felt so abandoned on the sidewalk where he'd left me. *You're not even human,* I wanted to fling at him. *You're like some kind of programmed robot—what's happened to you?* And then, *You're right; you are a fucking freak.*

17

t was all over the news by nine-thirty. I'd heard sirens wailing in the distance on that terrible walk home, but if they'd been on their way to the car dealership I'd assumed they were headed there to deal with the bomb threat. We'd phoned them in time; I didn't see how there could have been people on the lot as early as eight-thirty.

Mole and Cathy had the TV on. The news reporters were live from the scene, though cordoned off across the street. They kept asking their colleagues in helicopters if they had a clearer view of anything, but the aerial footage coming back from the choppers showed only the billows of thick black smoke. Ground cameras filmed the helicopters and vice versa, so that in lieu of more explicit shots of what they were supposed to be covering, the news media kept busy filming themselves.

"Oh, Jesus. Was anyone there?" I asked as I took a seat beside

Neil on the floor. My anger at him drained upon seeing the television images, and his ashen face.

"I don't know. Maybe," Mole said. "There were ambulances that
went to the scene and then left again."

"I'm sure they came automatically," I said. "That would make
sense. It doesn't mean that anyone was hurt. No one would have
been around at that hour, would they? It was eight-thirty.
Dealerships don't open at eight-thirty." I heard myself prattling,
but I couldn't stop.

"What have they said?" Neil asked.

"Only that a bomb threat was called in from a pay phone at the
university"—Mole shot us a look—"minutes before the explosion
at the dealership."

Cathy dropped her head in her hands and Mole put his arm
around her.

Scraps of the woman reporter's voice made her way to me
through my daze: ". . . several national and northwest environmental groups, headquartered here in Eugene . . . the device, apparently timed to go off before the dealership opened . . . caller did
not identify any organization." Then Mole flipped channels and a
man's voice cut in: ". . . firefighters from all districts in Eugene and
Springfield are at the scene . . . no suspects named at this time . . .
investigation under way."

I didn't say anything, nor did anyone, for a long time as the
reports repeated themselves and the little that was known. The
fire had been quickly brought under control. It was a practice to
keep the gas tanks of cars on the lot nearly empty as a fire precau-
tion. Maybe this was going to be okay, merely a wake-up call to
the SUV-owning public as Mole and Neil had planned.

Then, on another channel, a reporter, standing in front of the Emergency Room entrance at Harding Memorial Hospital: ". . . victim was thirty-six-year-old Michael Woodrow of Eugene, a salesman who apparently had reported early for work this morning at Benito Ford."

All the channels had a reporter at the ER now, and as Mole flipped around we heard the same bits over and over—extent of the injuries not known, apparently the sole victim of the attack—until finally one reporter cornered a paunchy middle-aged man in a sports shirt, identified by his caption as Larry Burton, general manager of Benito Ford.

"Mick's a great guy, one of our best salesmen," he said, choking up. He rubbed roughly at his eyes and continued in a firmer voice. "It isn't unusual for him to be first on the lot, open it up."

The reporter pressed him to say more about Michael Woodrow, tried to fish for more personal details, but Larry Burton just shook his head and said, "All our prayers are for Mick and his family now."

Little by little, data emerged. Michael Woodrow had a wife, a three-year-old son. He'd worked at Benito Ford for one year, been top salesman four of those twelve months. Everyone agreed—salesman Richard Gomez, salesman Daniel Wheeling—it wasn't unusual for Mick to show up before the showroom opened, catch up on paperwork so he could be available every minute on the selling floor. He'd been bested for Salesman of the Month in June by only four cars, and the guys had a friendly competition going for July. He was a great guy, a hard worker, a dedicated family man.

As the salesmen recounted Michael Woodrow's ambitions, I

saw him, coffee in hand, strolling through the showroom, stocking brochures, putting videos and toys in order in the kids' play area. Biding his time until it was time to go out and unhook the driveway chain. The balloons were bobbing, banners were snapping in a light breeze. A great day for selling cars. People felt optimistic when the sun was out, able to go that extra five thousand on their financing, more inclined to options like the stereo upgrade and the leather seats. Wasn't that how Mick Woodrow would figure it? Maybe he'd decided to open up early, be available in case an impulse browser wanted to pull in; that would be how to go about making Salesman of the Month.

His family didn't appear on TV, and I wondered if they'd been whisked into the hospital by a secret side entrance, since there would be no way they could avoid the gauntlet of reporters haunting the wide-springing automatic doors of the ER.

One station had managed to get hold of a photo of Woodrow already, maybe from the wife, or maybe from Larry Burton—wouldn't there be a mounted frame through which the beaming Salesmen of the Months rotated? Woodrow was young—not much older than I was—and killingly handsome, dark wavy hair, an expensive-looking suit to convey the message that no one was counting pennies here, not Mick Woodrow, not the customers coming in who might need to stretch a bit to make the payments. Good times, rising boats in a rising tide; that was the confident message his smile inspired.

We stayed glued to the television throughout the morning, no one thinking of lunch, and though some stations broke away to their regular Saturday kid fare, one hung doggedly with the story. Still no film of the wife, or of the three-year-old (for which I was grateful), but now Woodrow's balding, paunchy father was standing curbside in front of a modest ranch. He didn't look at the reporter as he talked, or at the camera. He looked toward the street, as if someone were there, Mick as a boy perhaps, riding a banana-seated Stingray. He told us Mick had never planned on selling cars for a living—at community college he'd taken mostly computer courses—but he'd fallen into this job and it had agreed with him. Told us that when his son matched a customer to the right car he felt he'd opened up something real for that person, helped them to their next big move in life.

"I just don't understand why—" He broke off to search the solemnly encouraging reporter's face. "Why anyone would—"

I left, then, to lie on the bed. I stared at the ceiling. No reprieve. No fortunate gap of fifteen minutes to make this merely a story of damaged cars and a dealer's losses.

Neil came in to lie down, and though he put his arms around me, my cue to turn to my side and burrow backward into his protective curve, I couldn't move. I couldn't bear the mock safety of our familiar nesting position. Better to be flat on my back, numb and exposed, corpselike. After a moment he removed his arm and rolled onto his own back and we remained there, confronting the blank ceiling, inches apart, lost.

18

eil and I hung around Eugene for three days, not daring to visit the Vine or go back to the forest. I could feel the protoplasm of our small cell drying up, disintegrating into nothingness.

On the second day Cathy took a friend to breakfast with her at the Vine and came back reporting that the headline on *Green Riot* crowed "SUV Bombing Strikes at the Heart of Detroit Terrorists!" though she was too afraid to pick it up and read the story or even to take a copy of the paper home with her. Mole said there were sure to have been FBI interviews with the regulars at the Vine and were probably undercover agents finding ways to listen in now.

He disappeared on the third night, to our surprise but not Cathy's, and at breakfast she invited us to leave, too—why not that day? I realized that in all likelihood I'd never see Mole again, just as I would probably never see any of the others back at the tree-sit. When we'd left the woods I'd assumed we'd be back for another stint, or at least to make a supply run. Mole and Neil had made several resupply trips there while I'd been working at Wainwright (an interlude that now seemed another life ago), but my ties were, it seemed, cleanly cut.

Now my losses seemed to be doubling, tripling, quicker than I could keep count. Neil and I agreed to reclaim our van and go; our improvised plan was to head to the coast. We didn't speak about what would happen after that. Maybe at the point we left we really didn't know, or maybe we just couldn't face it yet.

The van was just as we'd left it, parked in back of someone's house, a person we'd never actually met. Mole and Neil had used it a few times for their errands, but other than that we hadn't needed it. As far as we knew, the van was completely clean of movement ties. Our tent was in there, as well as our cooler and camp stove, artifacts of our trip out West when I'd still been able to pretend we were on vacation, celebrating the end of our school year and Neil's graduation.

We drove away from the Cascade forests, through rolling green Willamette Valley farmland that eventually rose up again to be the smaller evergreens of the Coast Range, where we once again encountered log trucks stacked high and festooned with red plastic ribbons on the ends of the fresh cuts. These were the harvests of managed forests, the logs pencil-thin compared to the girth of the old-growth trees we'd camped out in, and I flashed on the loggers' faces on my turn-of-the century postcards standing in deadpan triumph beside their monstrous trophies. The protest movements would never stop it, this need to *take*, to *own*, and I wondered when Neil would realize it.

If we'd killed Michael Woodrow—and we didn't know yet if we had or hadn't, they'd released no details by the time we left except to say that he was in critical condition, burns on thirty percent of his body, shrapnellike wounds complicating the burns—then we'd done so for nothing. I contended that not a single person would turn away from an SUV lot because of this, not one fewer Explorer would roll off Ford's assembly line. Probably we'd even harmed the movement, made it look crazy, extreme— lost the very sympathizers who might have joined with us. Mole, before he disappeared, had disagreed with me: He'd said that though he hadn't intended any casualties that night, the effect would be stronger for the violence we'd done. If people bought SUVs to feel bigger and safer, their families armored on the way to school and work against the vicissitudes of life, then we'd challenged that illusion on a very real level. Terrorism was effective, he'd argued, for its very randomness. Its arbitrary nature mirrored the capriciousness of life itself, only intensified, because you couldn't soothe yourself with the rational reassurance that no destructive force was out to get you in particular. But let's say the movement *was* out to get specific groups of consumers and producers—SUV drivers and makers, in this case; the fear of belonging to those groups would exponentially rise, because within the target groups was still the unnerving random element. Didn't I see?

I didn't, though Mole's delivery was maddeningly calm and reasonable. Because he seemed to bear no malice to anyone, his words were all the more frightening. Maybe people *would* postpone buying their new SUV for a week or a month, I'd countered, but they'd forget and go back. Was it worth the wrong of grievously wounding—maybe killing—a person? Did he intend on keeping the terror effect in play by planting a bomb a month? At which point Mole had looked up at me and said quietly, "Go home, Emerald. You don't belong here," and though I'd fully intended on going home, I was stung by his dismissal. I'd put more on the line than many. I'd also accepted full responsibility for being present that night, though I hadn't actually done anything except worry and wait.

Neil had been sitting with us in the living room, sipping an iced tea, but said nothing. He'd said practically nothing on the subject since the explosion, and I knew him well enough to assume that he was thinking and feeling his way through this. The economist in him might be persuaded by Mole's cost-benefit analysis, but what about the man? We still hadn't circled back to the substance of our Saturday morning fight, and I couldn't be sure how much he was prepared to sacrifice for his ideals; if he'd draw any lines based on questions of human worth.

We tailed the logging truck for two or three miles in a winding no passing zone, until Neil stomped on the accelerator and passed it on an almost-blind curve. There happened to be no car coming toward us at fifty miles an hour, but Neil couldn't have known that.

"Do you want me to drive?" I said.

"If I want you to drive, I'll ask."

"Please don't kill us, then."

"I have no intention of killing anyone," Neil said.

And because this was true enough, but obviously insufficient to keep us—or anyone—safe from Neil's lack of intention to kill them, the silence around us settled heavily.

Florence was a working fishing town, a place of no pretensions, where even the tourist industry was poky and halfhearted—a few billboards for dune buggy rentals, a couple of gift shops that sold seashell kitsch. We mostly slept in the cheap motel room I rented for us, and when we weren't sleeping, we ate. We kept our car parked in the motel's gravel lot and walked to our meals, steaming bowls of chowder with slicks of butter, the oyster crackers bobbing on top like buoys. We feasted on berry pie for dessert, asking for it heated and topped with ice cream. If the waitresses in the diner we favored came to recognize us, they didn't try to get friendly, we were so clearly our own, closed unit. We watched old movies from our motel bed and flicked to the news for updates on Michael Woodrow and the investigation. Even in the *Oregonian*, which we bought from the box outside our room, details were scarce. He was out of intensive care, which meant he would live. Since it was no longer a question of life or death, and since the smoke had cleared and the rubble had been cleaned up and there was nothing more for the news stations to film, he was fading from their story lineup.

Though I didn't, for obvious reasons, want to keep any clippings or old papers around, I couldn't help but fixate on a photo of Michael Woodrow that they'd put in the paper and flashed on the news. In it he was holding his son, Zachary, a small version of himself. Father and son had their cheeks pressed together and were grinning at someone who could have only been the wife. I felt the whole circle of their family life in that photo—how those grins were special for the picture taker, how she would have seen the two of them in a moment of horseplay and commanded them to hold still. When the media asked her for a picture, Jan Woodrow would have chosen that one as a message to us, the perpetrators. *See,* she was saying as she offered up that image of their private life, *see what you've done?*

A wonderful father, Michael Woodrow—who disagreed? It was documented in the papers, in quotes offered by all who knew him. Mick Woodrow had left his house before Jan and Zachary were up. That much was a known thing, one of the facts bobbing in colorless preservative, something his wife told the papers. Though it was he who had to go sell cars early on a Saturday morning, he might have felt like someone escaping, picking his way through the dark, toy-littered living room. All he had to do was talk to people all day, being himself—charming Mickey, everyone said so—drink his coffee and shoot the breeze with the guys in between customers.

I have imagined a hundred different narrative vessels to transport Michael Woodrow through the first hours of his Saturday morning, some of them docking safely: He sleeps in, or stays put behind the desk of his office instead of touring the lot, or he hears the squawk of a police radio in the showroom when he's in the bathroom taking a shit, pants slumped around his ankles. Any of those courses would have offered safe passage. But instead, something draws him outside. The rows of gleaming cars are a beautiful bait on a beautiful morning, and any minute now he'll have some tentative shopper swerving in to have a look, and he knows how to handle that, how to let that person have all the space he or she needs. There'll be lots of time for small talk and low-key inquiries about the customer's tastes and price range. He's good at relating to customers; this has been stressed in interviews, and I can see it in his eyes—a guy's guy young enough to know what it means to want a truck to go off-roading for the sheer hell-raising pleasure of it, but also a settled family man: He can look squarely at any parent and feelingly discuss security and dependability. He tells the moms that he's a father himself; the proof is in seeing him collapse a stroller or buckle a car seat in ten seconds flat. Mick would know how to telegraph the safety issue with a slap on the side panel, a careful salting of adjectives like *rugged* and *reliable*. He would confide that the Explorer is the car he drives and that his wife has her own to match, each with a car seat in the back for their three-year-old son.

Something compelled him outside to the lot: When? When Neil and I were jogging to the phone? Or later—one minute, two—just after the phone call was made? Did I personally waste that minute, squandering seconds to test Neil's character, arguing to see if he'd go with me?

But Michael Woodrow *is* outside, in that whole candy store of cars completely unmarred and unlittered, all cleaner than any new owner will ever be able to get them again. It is still a whole world; nothing has exploded, though I've run out of safe endings and am left with only a series of imaginings that lead to the appallingly actual. Does something beckon his attention over to the precise row where the bomb is hidden, its timer's needle lodged between one second and the next, hindered by a piece of dust or a bead of moisture? Mick stops before a pretty silver Explorer, deluxe and power everything, leather seating and sports trim. He notices that the placard in the windshield has slipped down. It's no big deal, really, but it looks askew in the perfect landscape of the lot, so he jogs inside for the key and back out again to pop the locks and nudge the placard up straight. Everything ideal. Odometers at zero, fresh slate, ladies and gentlemen, step right up to a new chapter in your life.

Mick casts a critical glance at himself in the passenger-side mirror, decides to button the bottom button on his polo shirt, then slams the Explorer's door.

I wondered if business was going on as usual at Benito Ford. They would have removed the peripherally damaged vehicles and filed their insurance claims. They would have reparked their remaining stock in pleasingly even rows. Though they might have had a picture of Michael Woodrow in the window while he lay hooked to respirators in intensive care, they would have quietly pulled it down now so there would be no unpleasant reminder to the customers who were no doubt trickling back. Perhaps a few diehard "Americans," the kind who bumper-sticker their cars with flags and slogans like SAVE THE SPOTTED OWL—FOR TARGET PRACTICE would have come out to trade in their trucks whether they needed to or not, just to show solidarity with American manufacturing and the freedom to choose—vehicles, that is. Maybe the dealership even experienced a bump in sales.

On the third morning I felt the need to shake free of the lethargy that had possessed us. We'd only made love once since we'd been at the beach, and that time had had a certain perfunctory nature to it we'd never experienced before.

"Do I tell them in the office that we're leaving or staying?" I asked at ten, getting out of bed to pull on my cutoffs, rummaging in my pack for my wallet. We'd already watched *I Love Lucy* and *Petticoat Junction* back to back. I didn't want to get back in that bed anymore—we'd spent hours there, and it was full of crumbs and powdered sugar from our morning donuts. "We could always drive up north, the beaches are supposed to be great."

"What do you want to do?" Neil asked.

"How about Cannon Beach?" I rose to open the opaque curtains a few inches. Neil wasn't dressed yet, but I couldn't take the gloom any longer.

"No, I mean what do you want to *do?*" he asked, rising up on his elbows.

I sat on the edge of the bed and met his eyes. Papers and clothes had littered the floor since we'd checked in, hanging our DO NOT DISTURB sign, and for once I hadn't had the urge to pick up after either of us.

"What do you want?" I asked in return.

"I'm going back to Eugene. You know that."

I chewed my lip for a minute, trying to think of something to say that wouldn't make this final.

He reached out and touched my arm, smiling slightly. "I do love you, you know," he said as if he'd refuted it earlier, or as if he'd never quite believed it himself.

As soon as he said it like that, I couldn't quite believe it, either. Though I had.

"Well, so, you're going back," I said, moving away from him, because with his last words something had crumbled in me. "I applaud you. Go back and work in the movement—they need people as smart as you. But why do you think that being an activist means becoming a terrorist?"

It felt important to say that word to him, make him hear it and decide for himself if it fit. I was clear-headed, remarkably so. His fate was his own, though I wanted to influence him if I could.

"You could still write and publish, you could still work for an agency, you could still fight for every single thing you believe in. Or do you want to be a terrorist?"

It seemed to me that I was putting the question very forcefully and clearly, leaving no room for obfuscation.

"You're being reductive," he said. "*Terrorist* is just a word. *Action, movement, protest, resistance, self-defense*—those are words, too. I could argue that they're more accurate ones."

"You could," I said. "But you'd still be a terrorist. Or a murderer. Someone almost *died*, Neil. Doesn't that bother you at all? Don't you think about it?"

"I do think about it. We didn't intend it." He spoke wearily, patiently, as if to a child. It occurred to me that I was very sick of people in the movement addressing me as if I were six whenever I questioned them.

"But when you plant bombs, it doesn't matter what your *intentions* are. Bombs have a habit of going off. And not always as planned."

"Obviously."

"Damn it"—I wanted to shake him—"will you quit patronizing me? You mean you can actually live with that?"

"Julie." He leaned close. Took my hands. I smelled how stale our clothes were, how sour his breath had become lately. "We're dying. We're all fucking dying because of ozone depletion and global warming and the systematic destruction of species and habitats. Try to tell anyone that in this country and you'll get laughed at, or categorized as a kook. Put it in a dissertation and its academic orthodoxy gets scrutinized, but not the message. Not the truth of it.

Work for policy change and you spend your life poring over sentences, changing commas and clauses by committee, meeting with bullshit politicians who couldn't give a flying fuck about anything besides their poll numbers. Meanwhile, Wainwright clearcuts. Automakers and manufacturers don't cap CO_2 emissions. This is death coming at us on a scale so much larger than a single car salesman. I'm sorry about him, I really am, but I'm willing to count him as a casualty and move forward. Believe me, I'm not trying to spread death around. Just the opposite."

I didn't have anything to say. I was tired of words. They didn't seem to lead me around to anything I could hold on to, anything that felt sound.

"Checking out, then," I said, withdrawing my hands.

He shrugged and lay back on the bed, signaling how absolute his will, how futile it was to try to move his judgment. He'd think things through himself, slowly and carefully and complexly, to be sure, but with no room for anyone else's opinion, and certainly not emotions. I mattered little to him in his intellectual arrogance. That is, my mind mattered little. I knew that when my body was no longer there to reach for in the dark, he'd suffer. I'd suffer, too, but whether it would be from love or needing to feel needed, I was no longer sure.

He lay still as I turned away, leaving the gloom for the gray but somehow dazzling contrast of an Oregon downpour, the green bushes at the edge of the parking lot rain-slicked and glowing with a life so insistent that I immediately felt the force of a furious headache skewering my vision. This air was too salt, too raw to breathe. I almost retreated back to the cavelike safety of the room, the warm stuffiness of our tangled breaths. Neil might have heard me pause on the sidewalk just outside our door. I wanted him to divine how unprotected I felt, how dizzy and alone, how almost sick to my stomach from the sudden onset of the headache, how in need of him to emerge and lead me back to bed, the darkness we'd sheltered in.

19

When I flew out of the Portland International Airport on a bright morning in early August there seemed to be not a single cloud from Oregon to Massachusetts. I spent hours studying the folds and ripples and crags and cookie-sheet flats of the country. The perspective was blinding—I could see nothing but shape and contour, nothing but a palette of silvered grays to greens, laced with occasional ink-colored waters. Rather than make conversation with the benign-looking stranger in the D seat—his open, ready-to-chat expression as he helped the flight attendant hand over my meal—I pressed myself to the lozenge of window, its two Plexiglas panes holding fast against the vacuum of emptiness outside.

It was as if I had to recover every inch I'd crossed over more than two months earlier with Neil, the landscape so much bigger and more mysterious in its long shadows than I'd been able to imagine from the point of view afforded by our rectangular campsites.

I was filled with a privacy I hadn't experienced in a long time, a space where my thoughts ran freely in any direction at all—like wisteria—blooming and trailing and winding itself over existing structures, but not bound by them, not of them.

Great round platters of farm country slid past underneath me, intersected by licorice strips of highway, ribbons of destination. The world was vast and intricate and unknowable, a thought that didn't overwhelm but comforted me, letting a heavy individual burden slip away. I could try to live in it lightly. Despite the jet fuel I was at this moment a party to consuming, the urban hive I was returning to, I didn't automatically do harm just by breathing, just by being Julie Prince. Or at least I didn't have to. *Harm* was a word persecuting my sleep now, a blade edged with two sides: the harm of doing nothing, the harm of trying to do good too desperately, too narrowly.

I had prayed for Michael Woodrow, not only that he would survive, but that he would survive to enjoy his life, his scars not disfiguring, his family life not unbearably damaged. I dreamed one night that I'd stolen his little boy—we were all in court, and I don't know if it was I who was being arraigned, or Neil, or Mole, or even Michael Woodrow, who never faced me to show me the extent of the injuries. In the dream his toddler had been unattended for some reason, and I had stolen the child and run. Then I'd woken up and had prayed for forgiveness from the dream.

Now that I'd prayed, was I a believer? Could I entrust myself to some healing, forgiving power that resided—somewhere? Everyone prayed sometimes, of that I'd become sure. It either meant nothing, or everything. Either such an impulse was merely the yearning of the human imagination to be mothered into infinity, or it was the indestructible memory that we were, in fact, cared for.

I didn't for a minute believe that Michael Woodrow had lived as a result of my prayers. Even at the time of making them, I'd known they couldn't have had that kind of power. Yet he had lived, and that was the main, the only, thing. Perhaps it was the love of his wife or son that had pulled him back, his determination not to leave them, and so maybe that was the answer—no God but in the ties binding us, the willingness to imagine others' need and answer it. Clearly Neil and I had failed that test. If I'd been able to believe in his love, if he hadn't referred to it in the end in such a self-canceling way—I *do* love you, you know—what might have happened? As it was, we merely drove north up 101 together, stopping for walks in Newport, Depot Bay, Cannon Beach, taking our time because neither of us had anywhere pressing to be.

We made love when we checked into our last motel, a fancy three-story one in Cannon Beach, some of the force that had drawn us together that first night in April returning. There was anger in it, too; at the time I wouldn't have said it was anger with each other, but now I see that it must have been. Afterward, we slept pressed together, every part that could touch touching, and then made love again in the morning, more gently, more forgivingly, just before fully coming awake.

"You don't have to go," he said, his mouth to my ear, his words caught in my hair. "Don't go, J."

Instead of an answer, I kissed him lightly on the forehead, and got up, naked, warm, to make coffee in the room's kitchenette. I'd insisted on getting us an ocean view this time, no dingy little box of a room to remember as the last night. I intended to make an answer, but it hadn't taken shape yet. I wanted to give it the space of this large room to move about in, the vista from this floor-to-ceiling plate glass looking down on the stunningly blue Pacific as it broke into surf around the intractable presence of Haystack Rock. We'd left the drapes and glass door to the balcony open all night to let in the sea air, and now a couple of gulls landed on the other side of the screen to mutter about their hunger.

If I gave them one morsel from our bag of breakfast pastries they'd come by the dozens, by the hundreds, to demand all that we had. To protest and decry our barrenness once we'd run out of crumbs.

"Goodbye, birds," I said, sliding the door closed.

Look at the room my grandfather's money could buy, how it could let the radiance of a whole ocean spill onto our bed.

I didn't have to go.

While the coffee hissed and dripped, its smell wafting in and out of my perception like cartoon fingers of scent, I sat cross-legged on the bed, glorying in my nakedness, the gift I made of it to his staring. His arms were crossed behind his head on the two down pillows covered with starched linens.

I let myself forget that we had only four hours remaining in this privacy and light, let myself be happy. He was there at my pleasure—naked, too, above the covers—and I examined him, the dark stubble of his chin, his almost black hair fanned out against the bunched pillows. I'd never told him that I first fell in love with his smell. The curling hair in his armpits was bleached a shade lighter than the rest of his body hair from the strength of his sweat, as if something corrosive inside him had to find its outlet there. But the intensity of it was like the best intensity of him, the code of pheromones in it addressed personally to me.

"I love your smell," I said softly. "That's what I loved first."

He grabbed me by the hands and pulled me onto him. "I love your cunt," he whispered, and I was used to the way he said that word by now, the hard reverence of it. "I love your breasts, and your hair, and your skin, and your tongue, and the way you say everything—the sound of your voice filling me up. I love your little ears," he said, then thrust his tongue into one, so that he couldn't say more, nor could I hear it if he did, only feel the jolt of current he sent through me. We made love again—worthy, that time, of our elevated setting—in full consciousness of the light, eyes open to each other the whole time.

Then coffee, in two ceramic mugs we could wrap our fingers around, dressed and sitting side by side on the balcony, watching people make their thin tracings near the hem of the sea as they ran, or walked dogs, or took a morning stroll. They didn't have the view we did of their smallness.

"You might come back to Boston," I offered.

He nodded once, barely acknowledging the truth of this.

We sipped hot coffee in silence, and I tried, but failed, to imagine him living with my money, instead of merely taking holidays in its company, as he had been. Or we could live like graduate students; I wouldn't have to use it.

But he wasn't a graduate student anymore, so what would he be? And I?

"Mole said I wasn't cut out for it, the stuff you need to do."

"I think we all know that," he said gently.

By *all* did he mean everyone I'd worked with in the movement?

Starling and Mudman and Spiderman? Even inconsequential little Squirrel? Was it so obvious to anyone who knew me just a little?

I determined that he meant Mole, himself, and me, our cell. I'd been fond of the intimacy of that word, thinking only of living, pulsing things in connection with it. Not of prison, that imitation burial, a stone and steel vault whose walls you could touch on either side by standing in the middle and stretching arms out.

"It's just that it's so stupid to end this way," I blurted. "We're not mad at each other, right? We're not out of love . . . or harmony, or sympathy. . . ."

Neil bent forward and said, "We're not out of anything," and held my eyes so long that I knew it was hopeless.

We used every minute that was coming to us and then stole a few more, staying half an hour past the checkout time. A breeze came up, chilling the air and pushing clouds over the sun, but we remained on the balcony, keeping warm under the bedspread we'd dragged out. There was no thought of having more sex. Sex had done all it could for us. We sat with shoulders touching under the quilt, in the way of old couples who had long since reckoned with every failing the other had, and still remained side by side at the end, claiming the same view.

Then he drove me to Portland and my airline reservation, and though he wouldn't take any money for the ride back down I–5 to Eugene, he did agree to let me top off the gas tank. Later he would have found the five twenties I folded into his wallet when he went to use the bathroom.

No one met me on the other side. I hadn't phoned my mother

since the message I'd left her on her machine on my birthday. The bombing had made national news; she'd left me half a dozen worried messages in the days since it occurred, wondering where I was and when I was going to call, but I couldn't respond to any of them.

I walked through Logan feeling a pressure in my chest almost equal in intensity to what I'd felt on the night of Benito Ford. How had I managed to arrive squarely back here, in the nonworld of this familiar silver and white airport, the unearthly ball-and-chute sculpture clinking and tinkling as the balls ran down the scales, drawing children like moths to press against its glass. I, too, had loved passing by that ingenious machine on my trips back and forth from Boston. Now, for a reason I couldn't name, its mechanistic certainties—inexorable proof of cause and effect, momentum and hurtling velocity—seemed menacing.

20

At home, I rang the buzzer instead of letting myself in. Don't ask me why. Maybe to spare my mother a shock too sudden, for as it was, she couldn't stop trembling the whole first evening. I didn't have much to say for myself, and after the first hug, which felt all wrong to me—my arms used to a different shape—I kept a space between us, though she kept reaching across it to touch me on the arm or stroke my hair. I tried to let her, but each time I found myself edging away. She was doing her best, I could see, not to hover or encroach. But the energy of her love and relief surging toward me was exhausting, and I stayed for only a few days before I told her I needed to go visit Frida and her family at the Cape for a week.

Once I was with Frida I started to feel more like myself. Over drinks on the deck I gradually told a version of my summer—the forest part, the hanging around Eugene part, the Neil part. She didn't press, she didn't interrogate—her listening was like a cool swim in a lake. Frida had her own stories to tell about the pierced biologist, her internship in Boston, and I relaxed into her company, feeling safe for the first time in a long while. When September came we went back to Wellesley, its acres of obscene lush privacy, its trails and pond, its moneyed, artfully natural sprawl.

I changed my schedule to mainly art classes, back to painting after a three-year hiatus. I remember those two semesters as mainly a time of feeling the power of color, the language of brush-strokes, the tactility of paint. It was my senior year and, dutiful student that I'd been in the previous three, I could fill it with electives. My only non-art class was Contemporary Poetry, and I read the poets silently, fiercely, and wrote nothing of my own.

Senior year, I went to no more parties of the kind where I'd met Neil—not one. I was like one of those older returning students who come to Wellesley after great stretches of life experience, who go quietly about the business of finishing their educations while being viewed, in the eyes of the other students, as mysteriously inward figures, long since immune to the urgent social concerns that shape normal undergraduate life.

I lived quietly, but not placidly. It was always in the back of my mind that I'd given my name and Social Security number to Wainwright Timber. Despite the warnings of Mudman, Spiderman, Starling, and Mole, I had brazenly—to no real purpose, it now seemed—put myself in the open. Once in a while I Googled Michael Woodrow, but there was nothing beyond a short article in the *Register-Guard* that he was now recuperating at home. He'd had skin grafts and would require more. The newspaper said the investigation had yielded nothing so far, but I knew enough not to trust statements the authorities made to the media. They might have made some connections, been slowly stringing facts together.

I graduated, on time, with my class. I was able to look as festive as the rest as we threw our tasseled caps into the air, as I posed beside my mother, then Frida, then Preston. I ate my celebratory lobsters, bibbed like an infant. I raised my glass. My mother wanted to know what I'd like for a gift—something serious, something fitting—and I told her I'd let her know. The truth is, I was stymied by a lack of desire. I didn't crave travel or things, didn't need a car beyond the battered Honda I bought used my first year of college and had been driving since.

My mother had apparently declared a moratorium on questions. She didn't dare wonder aloud what my next move would be, or demean my new job to me, though I'm sure she fretted aloud to Preston. I didn't tell her it was only temporary, the one thing that would have allowed her to relax. I wanted her to struggle to accept that this might be who Julie was, what Julie did. The children I taught at Hillside Children's Center reminded me of Zachary Woodrow. I saw him in the boys that came whizzing down the play yard blacktop on their riding toys, their sneakered toes dragging them to a stop at the yellow line. I helped them paste painted macaroni to construction paper and read them flannel board stories, "Three Billy Goats Gruff" the one they never seemed to tire of.

Frida was the one in law school now, funny, funky Frida with her tattooed ankle. She complained about the mountains of work, the competitive students, the grind of it all, but I could see that she loved it, just like Ginnie. There were some mothers at

Hillside who thrived on their work and others who were torn apart by it. The ones who loved it didn't have that furtive, hunted look as they left. You felt them merge back into the adult world with pleasure as they stepped outside our crayoned and collaged room, searching in bags for their keys and phones. The others lingered a few beats too many, and some invisible regret jumped from them to their children, who became clingy and anxious until they finally departed. It had occurred to me that I wasn't just finding Zachary Woodrow in the room, but maybe some long-ago version of me, in Charlotte or Thalia over there in the dramatic play corner as they bossed each other over how to use the props and dress-up. I really wanted those torn-apart mothers to be at once a little brisker and a little more reassuring as they took their morning's leave. And I saw that for the other ones—the Ginnies—it wasn't really a choice. To give up what they did all day in the adult world and trade it for our clay and paint was simply not thinkable.

Charlotte and Thalia were happy. They spent whole days being happy under my care and that of the other teachers, and I remembered with surprise that I had been a happy child, too. I had nothing much to forgive my mother for.

I planned to do this a while longer because I liked it. A year had passed and I hadn't grown bored yet. The children had so much to offer, so much wisdom and curiosity. I laughed a lot when I was with them. But it was a detour for me, not a life.

In the evenings after work I went through everything I'd ever drawn or painted or made, mentally trying to construct a portfolio that might convey a seriousness of purpose and a modicum of talent. Mostly I did this in the privacy of my room, but sometimes when I was standing in front of the clay nudes that my mother had enshrined on the mantel, or one of my paintings that she had framed and hung in the hallway, trying to decide whether slides of them were worth including in an application to art school, she would catch sight of me and make some approving remark, like, "Oh, I *love* that one," or "I'm so glad to see you're thinking of an MFA." Then I suddenly saw the whole thing as ridiculous. I'd had the forms for weeks, downloaded from the Internet, and if I was serious I should have been going about getting slides made and contacting recommenders from Wellesley, but a kind of paralysis overtook me and I began to doubt I'd ever go through with this. Here's what I feared, and maybe believed: that I was good enough to know what good art was, but not good enough to ever make it myself. Just because I was rich (not by *Forbes* standards, but pretty much by the rest of the world's), did that mean I had the right to indulge these fantasies about myself? To spend my days making art that only my mother would end up displaying because I thought it was *fun?*

Frida brought me men regularly, like a mother bird dangling tasty bits over the nest. She had an endless supply of bright male buddies from law school, and she tried to invite the more socially aware ones over to her Cambridge apartment for little soirees, where I felt myself presented with all the variety and quality one could wish for. I loved Frida, and I loved her even more for her efforts, like introducing me to John, with his brown curls and specialty in environmental law, and there was no reason that I should have failed to appreciate his sincere and public-spirited interests. But I found myself unable to lift my eyes for long above the shoulder line of his claret-colored cashmere sweater to maintain eye contact. I felt his gaze searching my face with an interest that wasn't merely polite, yet I was too distracted by the understated good taste of his sweater to reciprocate. My sheer inability to ask him anything about himself, or volunteer anything about myself, or have much of an opinion on anything eventually drove him away, as I'd intended it to.

Why blame a man for wearing a nice sweater? It wasn't as though I'd dressed myself in rags for Frida's party. I went in a pretty white peasant blouse with flared sleeves edged in cotton lace, a woven wool skirt the color of moss. Around my neck hung the medicine bag from Cody, and when people asked me what it held, I said, as I always did, "Nothing." The children were the only ones I'd ever shown the twig of Maia to. Sometimes they asked to pass it around at circle time, each of them holding it with tremendous care, and I'd tell them again how when the great tree was still a little shoot America wasn't yet America, it was a place where Native Americans lived and had different names for their land in different languages. I'd tell them that some of those languages have been forgotten, though the tree must have heard them (words buried in the first rings of its heartwood), and that it grew for all those hundreds of years in silence, its branches extended to hold many kinds of creatures. Then they'd ask me if the tree was still there, and I'd say yes, hoping.

I would see news of Maia's cutting, if it ever happened, on the Forest Warriors' website, which I'd checked every week or so since returning. Tree-sitters had occupied Maia continuously for three years, unnoticed by most of the world. My heart bumped when a new photo had been scanned in, and I'd enlarge the page, trying to decide if any of the tiny, bandanna-masked figures in the tree or on the ground were Neil. I'd enlarge until the faces dissolved in a puzzle of pixels, but I never found him.

Every now and then I'd get a postcard, unsigned, of someplace we'd been together—Baker Park, the U of O campus. They all said the same thing: *Weather's fine, wish you were here.* This was a code I understood. That he was safe, for now. That he missed me the way I missed him, in a way that made sleep our only possible reunion, from which I could wake crying out from actual orgasm, sure that my arms had just been holding on to something solid. He signed with one x, one o. He couldn't write news, he wouldn't complain of loss or pretend that we'd see each other again. I understood all of this. He couldn't be sure, either, that I hadn't moved beyond him, to someone like John of the claret-colored sweater. He wouldn't give me a way to get in touch with him, for the safety of us both. That the telegraphic lines he wrote had such a power to move and inform me, that they resounded with meaning only I could discern, testified to the connection we still had. If the connection died, the words would harden into their polished surface, harmless cliché, which, one day, I might barely read and toss away.

When my mother was the one to collect the mail, she passed the cards to me without comment. Living at home was one of those things I did temporarily, glad that I could give my mother pleasure from an act so passive. Once she said something startling to me at dinner, something without preamble or explanation. "I know something about love, Julie." That was all. I was too shocked to ask her what—*what* it was she knew—but I was certain she wasn't talking about her love for me. I flashed on Preston's face, maybe intuiting something more about her feelings for him than she'd ever admitted to me. Didn't I sometimes have a queasy feeling seeing my mother perched on a chair in their living room, Harvey stretched out on the enormous brown couch like a bearded pasha, reading the *Times*, while Preston hummed in the kitchen, caramelizing the onions? Did I only ever imagine something fallen in her face as she gamely accompanied the two of them to pick out a new lamp? There was a photo of Preston with Ginnie at their law school graduation, my mother's hand resting on his forearm, on the coppery fur that grew lightly there. This was before Harvey was on the scene. Wouldn't you say that a woman would tilt her head just so only toward a man she loved? They had told me, and I believed, that Preston was not my father. But—*I know something about love, Julie*—was it possible that he had ever been my mother's lover? Or the one she would have chosen if she could? Maybe my mother's words had been an offering, a readiness to share something, but at the time I could only look away.

I knew something about love, too. I'd called it everything—need, lust, use—but finally, I was just calling it love. It didn't end when it ended, it didn't *bend with the remover to remove*. Just because you knew something was behind you, and that you'd never get it back, didn't mean you were finished with it, or ever would be.

21

What signifies an end? How far does an action carry its consequence into the future, like the butterfly in Beijing whose wing brushes the air into a ripple that will ripen to a hurricane in Mexico?

The bomb that went off last night at Wainwright Timber in Eugene, Oregon, ripping the building apart, and the secondary blaze it produced, leveling most of what remained, left no casualties. The building was empty. (Marcia, you were at home. Can Matthew, two, climb out of his crib yet? Had he come to your bed from a bad dream, prying a space between you and Dave?) No group claimed responsibility for the blast. (Verna, your reading glasses were on the nightstand. Did you stay up late, trying to finish a novel in time for your reading group? When your bulletin board of grandchildren was incinerated, were you comfortably unconscious, wrapped in the warm flannels of late middle age?)

And where was I? More than two years distant from my dishonest presence among them, waking three hours ahead of their time zone, maybe showering at the moment of the blast, to go to my job at Hillside. I would find out from the evening news, a two-minute story sandwiched between continuing reports of the World Trade Center investigation, and the endless profiles of those survivors as they faced their first Thanksgiving.

Police say the explosion at Wainwright Timber is probably the work of local environmental groups long embattled with area foresters and unrelated to Al Qaeda or other foreign terrorist organizations.

And where were you, Mole? I've hoped that the maps I drew (that so delighted you) of the entire building's layout have been long rubbed into unreadable scraps, riding the back pocket of your jeans for all these months. Maybe what I told you had nothing to do with your planning. Maybe I was so inconsequential to your thinking that if someone interviewed you right now about a person named Emerald and her involvement as an accessory to your crime, you'd draw your brows together in genuine puzzlement and say, "Who?," the needle on the lie detector graph staying straight and even.

It's implausible that Verna and Marcia would think, this much later, that my anomalous presence among them bore any relation to the present misfortune. I doubt that my name will be brought up, even fondly, by them—"There was that girl—was it two summers ago?—who helped out for a month. We were sorry to lose her."

Only the payroll records, then, if they bother to comb through them. Only one fact to check that could give anything away: Is that girl still at the U? Then the lead turning hot after someone at the admissions office says, "What girl?"

What girl? The girl whose Social Security digits can be found in last year's IRS data, a Hillside Children's Center day-care teacher who filed her return on time.

All that was lost: stucco and plywood and roofing and insulation and glass and office machines and filing cabinets and paper. Only the materials necessary to the efficient functioning of Wainwright Timber as it seeks to overturn injunctions barring its execution of certain timber leases. Mr. Wainwright, is your son in the game yet? Are the two of you cursing whoever did this as you survey the damage? Did the varnished Chinook salmon, blown free of its trophy mount, survive the blast to be retrieved by you from its resting place in the parking lot, a Dadaist still life you wouldn't pause to appreciate? Mr. Wainwright would be on his cell right now to Amy, the bookkeeper, telling her, even as he toed the rubble, to order new checks; that everyone will continue to be paid. That's the kind of boss he is.

Eight weeks ago it was a brilliant morning and we had taken the children outside early. It was sunny, not yet officially fall; they didn't need coats. Helen, our director, came out and spoke to Rachel, the lead teacher in the Explorers' room. Rachel's hand flew to her mouth and stayed there. Rachel was frozen in place, so Helen moved from teacher to teacher in the play yard delivering whatever word she had that seemed to turn her staff into stone. When it was my turn I almost missed hearing what she said, because I was telling Robert not to throw wood chips into the air, they could get into Thomas's eyes.

As frantic parents called throughout the morning, Helen kept telling them our routines were continuing, their children were safe where they were and that they were unaware of anything unusual. I hugged my co-teacher, Lee, in the staff room, then we stuck to our planned theme of the solar system at morning circle time. Lee held the globe and I held the flashlight. She turned earth very slowly so the children could see where their counterparts on the other side of the world would be waking up for school just as they were home being tucked in for sleep. The lesson was a big hit, and the children kept coming up to us all day to ask: *Where on the earth are the children going to sleep now? Where are they waking up?*

Now we have potassium iodide locked away in the supplies cabinet. Helen spent the fall conferring with city officials and redrafting the emergency and evacuation plan. She invited a child psychologist to meet with parents for a discussion of the aftereffects of trauma on children.

Since hearing about Wainwright, I've searched the Forest Warriors' website for news of Neil, aka River, before I wondered, can they find out who visits a site? Can they follow my e-mail address back? I logged off and haven't gone on again.

The trickle of news from Eugene has disappeared in the great river of ongoing 9/11 reporting, unless I were to go online and read the *Register-Guard,* which for the moment I'm too afraid to do, imagining my presence in cyberspace as a bright dot, easily tracked. Maybe the investigation into Wainwright will be cut short, all the local resources poured into following the trail of Al Qaeda and its terrorist cells that might be tentacled everywhere, sleeping still.

Do I draw a distinction between the terrorist I told Neil he had become and what they are? I try to, thinking how death was their mission from the start, never Neil's, never mine. But a fuse is a fuse. It sputters to its irrevocable conclusion no matter what rationale you've given yourself for lighting it. Look at Michael Woodrow. He could so easily be dead right now, instead of nursing whatever wounds we left him with. Something in me won't rest until I actually see him, turn him from a story to a man, satisfy myself that he has a face, hands, can smile and talk. And if he can't? Is there any forgiveness for that?

And still, I want to be defended, if the knock on the door comes and it's for me. I've asked Preston to have lunch with me tomorrow. Before we begin, I'll tell him that I'm seeking legal advice. I haven't grown up with lawyers for nothing—whatever I tell him next will be privileged. I'll tell him everything: that I'm sorry, and afraid. I'll begin at the beginning, with my name, the one he doesn't know.

None of the children I teach had family members in the World Trade Center, or in the Pentagon, or on the plane over Pennsylvania. But you always know someone who knows someone. Living in the world is like that, a web of connection, a system of roots and branches. We turn in common on the planet, one minute bathed in light, the next in darkness. We go to sleep, and somewhere distant, someone rises to inherit the day we left undone.